D1257972

For Ruby and Her Friends.

In memory of Mike Lefiti
(affectionately known as "Big Mike")
1971–2017

Thank you to Rebecca Herman, Elena Lee and Laura Singer for their contributions.

Special thanks to Irv Santana for creating the surname Hoogablased, which is pronounced *Who-ga-blah-said*.

"MIRIAM: The Witch of Glen Park," Story and illustrations by Mark Shoffner
Additional drawings by Ruby Shoffner
Book design: Sean Riley

Juvenile Fiction: Humor, Fantasy, Witches, San Francisco
ISBN: 978-1-64440-319-8

Miriam
The Witch of Glen Park

By Mark Shoffner

Shenania Press • San Francisco

First of the Month

Miriam awoke early Saturday morning. The warm light was streaming through her window. Her cat, Frankie, was already awake. "Well, good morning, my dear," she said, stroking the cat's back. "Isn't this a fine morning? And where's Johnny?"

She scanned her little one-room apartment, looking for Johnny. "Where is that *w-w-wascally* cat?" she said in a funny voice.

Her gaze landed on a calendar sitting atop a stack of bills. "Oh, no. What day is it, Frankie?"

Miriam's happiness drained away. In its place was a sick feeling, right down in her stomach. April 1st was circled on the calendar. It was the First Day of the Month.

For weeks she had been dreading the arrival of the first of the month. Today her new rent was due: TWO THOUSAND DOLLARS a month for this tiny room on a noisy downtown street. And the landlord, Mr. Pappas, would be coming for it.

It wasn't fair, not fair at all. Miriam had lived here for more than a year, through good times and bad. And most recently times had been bad, *very* bad. Everything was going steadily downhill. First she had lost her job, then her health insurance. After that, she got sick. The landlord knew all of this, and still he was raising the rent. Again. He wanted to drive her out any way he could to make way for younger, richer tenants.

Miriam let out a sigh. None of her schemes had come to fruition, and now she would be homeless again. She looked down at her adoring cat, always by her side. "We'll make it somehow," she told Frankie. "Now go find your brother. I have something to tell you both."

Suddenly, there was a knock on the door. The knock turned into pounding. "Open up, Miriam!" said a voice from the hallway.

Already they are coming for the rent? Miriam had barely gotten out of bed. She hadn't even put on her glasses. She hadn't had time to think, or plan, or do anything. Would she be thrown out on the street, like so much trash?

"Oh. Why do I always wait till the last minute!" she said, looking desperately at her cats. "All my plans down the toilet."

Frankie and Johnny joined their whiny voices in a long, sad *meeeeow*. They completely agreed.

Chapter 2

Three
Angry Men

Miriam put on a robe. She tiptoed the ten steps from her bed to the front door. As quietly as she could, she peered through the peephole. Outside she saw Mr. Pappas in his red sweater. But it wasn't only Mr. Pappas. There were two other men, as well. Mr. Biddle, from the insurance company, said, "Open up!" And Mr. Lee was there, too. Oh, not Mr. Lee. He was the sheriff's deputy. It would be almost impossible to deal with all three of them at once.

Miriam took a moment to concentrate her thoughts. She focused her gaze on Frankie and Johnny, who awaited their instructions. She motioned silently toward the back of the apartment. The cats padded away. They understood what to do.

The three men pounded and pounded on the door. When there

was no answer, Mr. Pappas went downstairs to get the key. "You should have thought of that in the first place," said Mr. Biddle, who was very efficient himself. "Yeah!" said Mr. Lee, who seldom had an original idea of his own.

Mr. Pappas came back with the keys. "It's not this one," he said. "Not this one, either." He slid the last key into the door, saying, "This has to be the one."

The door sprang open, and all three tumbled into Miriam's apartment. "Wait. Where on Earth is she?" asked Mr. Pappas.

"She's gone? But I just saw her beady little eye through this peephole!" cried Mr. Biddle.

"Yes, it looks like she's gone," said Mr. Pappas, almost as if he had expected this to happen. "To be honest, she's always been a little… *witchy.*"

"Witchy? What's that mean?" asked Mr. Lee.

"Well, she's just strange, you know? No husband, few friends. Just cats, cats, cats…"

"Oh, well. I like cats," said Mr. Lee.

"You're missing the point!" yelled Mr. Pappas. "I mean, do you *talk* to cats? And do they *talk back*? And now, *poofus disappearus.* Like that, all three of them are gone, gone, gone."

The apartment was completely empty. All of Miriam's furniture, books, plants… all of it was gone. How had the old woman made her escape? There was no back door to the apartment. Mr. Pappas examined the single window, which was sealed up tight. There was no way that the rickety fire escape had been used, either. Had she just vanished into thin air?

"What's this?" asked Mr. Lee, wandering toward the back of the apartment. He found a greenish line traced on the bedroom wall. Mr. Lee pressed a plump finger against the wall, and found it moist. He kept pressing. His fingers went right through. A little crack of light streamed into the room. "Whoa…."

"What are you doing?" shouted Mr. Pappas. "That woman is probably halfway out of the city by now. We've got to go, go, go!"

Mr. Lee was a little taken aback. After all, he was an officer of the law and not used to being shouted at. He forgot about the hole in the wall as quickly as he had found it. Rearing up, he made a bold statement. "OK. No more Mr. Nice Guy. Let's bring her in, and LOCK HER UP!"

Chapter 3

The Street

Miriam, you see, was already down on the street. Quicker than seemed possible, she had put everything she owned into two medium-sized bags. She and her cats had slipped easily through the back wall of her apartment right into the stairwell, down the stairs, through the back door of the old building, onto the street.

"Okay... Frankie. And... Johnny," she said, out of breath. "I've told you this day might come. Now it's here, and we are *outta* here!" They hurried down Turk street, turning a corner.

It wasn't long before the angry men were down on the street, turning the corner after her. "Miriam Levin, your rent is still due, and there's the damage to the apartment, too!" yelled Mr. Pappas. "Your hospital bills are way past due," said Mr. Biddle. And Mr. Lee, who was always a little confused, said, "ME TOO!"

There was no way she could outrun all three of them. In a panic, Miriam crossed to the other side of the street, cars honking at her. Her cats followed closely behind—they knew their way around better than anyone.

Miriam kept running, but the men were gaining on her. She could practically feel Mr. Pappas's hot, garlicky breath on the back of her neck.

A block down, she spied a dark alley behind a Chinese restaurant. *That must be Dodgy Alley*, she thought to herself. It was risky to go down Dodgy Alley even in the daytime, but this was an emergency. She scurried around a parked car, and ducked down the alley. There she dove behind a pair of recycling bins. "Get in here!" she whispered to her cats.

Wow, what a smell behind those bins! It was the stench of sour milk and rotting vegetables. And there was something slimy under Miriam's leg. "What are we going to do?" she said, a little too loudly.

Everything got quiet again. Maybe the men had gone on by. Maybe they had missed the alley. Miriam relaxed a bit and pulled a long chow mein noodle from under her leg. She was still too nervous to stand up. Those men could be waiting for her in the alley. It seemed like something they'd do.

The recycling bins began to shake. She glimpsed a hand, and something red. It must be Mr. Pappas. Frantically, Miriam whispered to her cats, "I'm finished now, they'll take me to jail for sure. But you, my dears, you've got to run, run, RUN!"

The cats froze in place, though. They wouldn't leave Miriam's side, not without a hissing fight.

The hand was getting closer. It shoved the green composting bin to the side. There was nowhere to go. Miriam felt like a rat in a glue-trap.

Then she saw a face appear. It wasn't Mr. Pappas, or the other angry men. It was a cheerful looking woman in a bright red shirt.

"Well, HELLO in there," said the woman, smiling and nodding. "And how are YOU doing today?"

Miriam gave a long sigh. When the young lady asked the question again, Miriam didn't know what to say. After all, she was crouching behind a garbage can, sitting in a pile of Chinese take-out noodles and spilled milk, and this woman wanted to know how she was doing?

"I'm… fine, I guess?" said Miriam. It's the only response that came to mind.

The young salesperson reached forward to shake Miriam's hand. "Well, that's great! It's a pleasure to speak with you today. Now, I wonder if I can interest you in a *new smartphone*? We offer a complete package, with no roaming charges for people who are… housing challenged?" The saleslady wiped her hand and produced a shiny smartphone from her pouch.

"What? I'm not housing challenged, or homeless, or any such nonsense. I've lived here most of my life," said Miriam, angrily, fumbling in her bag. "It's true, I seem to be without a home *at the moment.*"

"I totally understand," said the lady, still smiling. "By the way, we have a special offer. If you pay a lot of money right now, you'll get a free month in two years!"

"Um… yes, that sounds just fine," said Miriam. She reached deep into her bag and came up with a long, yellowed piece of paper.

"What is that?" asked the saleslady, nervously. "Is it a competing offer from another company? I *guarantee* we can match it."

"Okay, okay. Just listen for a minute," said Miriam. She held up the paper and started to read in a low voice:

One woman's choice is another's curse,
Close your eyes or open them wide
Either way, there's no way to hide.
A thieving hand's inside your purse…

What was this crazy old woman talking about, the young lady wondered. Still, Miriam's soothing voice snuck up on her. She couldn't *not* listen. Soon, her eyes were glassy and vacant.

Miriam finished her strange poem. She put a hand gently on the young woman's shoulder, and leaned in to whisper in her ear. "You'd like to give me that nice smartphone now, right?"

"I'd like to give you that nice smartphone now, right?"

Without another word, Miriam grabbed the phone and set off down Dodgy Alley. The saleslady was still in a trance. Finally, she perked up and called after Miriam. "Wait! Is this a two-year contract? Five year? It's been a real pleasure connecting with you."

Miriam and her cats were already out of earshot. They were long gone.

Chapter 4

The Hoogablaseds

The Hoogablased family lived in a nice old house. The house was on a nice quiet street in the neighborhood of Glen Park. They had lived in their house for thirteen years, through good times and better times. And recently times had been good, *very* good. Everything was going steadily uphill. Mother and Father had started a new business called *Goober.com*. Their startup was a success, and soon they were raking in the money.

Through it all, Father and Mother's lives revolved around their daughters, Lucy and Ruth. They were loving children, even with their funny twin-sister ways.

On this particular morning, Harry Hoogablased awoke early, the warm sunlight streaming through the windows of the old house. "Rise and shine," he called up the stairs to his daughters. "Come on down, Lucy. Come on… Ruthie."

Soon the girls were filing down the staircase. Lucy came first in colorful heart themed pajamas. Then came her sister, Ruth, in tight black leggings.

It was time for breakfast, and each Hoogablased had a job to do.

Ruth got a cooking pot. Lucy took out the steel cut oats and some bowls.

"Where's mom?" asked Lucy. "It's Oatmeal Day. That's her favorite!"

"I'm right here," said Mother, cheerfully. She came in the back door, carrying a basket full of weeds. She gave Lucy a little squeeze. "I was out back trying to work on that garden."

"I could help in the garden," said Lucy with a smile. She looked over at her sister. "Maybe Ruthie would help, too?"

Her sister was not smiling. She was not in a cheery mood. "I have told you a million times. My name is not *Ruthie*. It's Ruth, plain and simple. Not everyone in this family has to have a cute little name like *Lucy* or… *Barbie*."

"Well," said Lucy. She was trying to think of something to say back. "Maybe I'll call you *Little Ms. Grumpy*, 'cause that's what you are."

"Oh, please," said Ruth. "Is that the best you can do?"

"Girls… girls," said Mother, carrying bowls of hot oatmeal to the table. "Let's try to get along on this beautiful day. Okay?"

Mother folded her hands, and looked around the table. She turned to Ruth. "Would you like to say grace, dear?"

Ruth didn't seem to be paying attention. Or she was putting all of her attention somewhere else. Suddenly, a flash of anger passed over Mother's face. "Ruth Ann Hoogablased, are you looking at that tablet under the table? You know today is device-free Saturday!"

"Ugh," said Ruth, looking up from her tablet. "Okay, I'm sorry. It just gets so boring without my tab...."

Ruth could see that her mother was still upset, so she walked over to the counter. She peered into the old dumbwaiter containing a basket of charging phones and tablets. She deposited her tablet next to the other forbidden devices. It was going to be a long Saturday....

Ruth slunk back to her chair. She pressed her hands together as everyone waited. She began, "Our lord, we thank you... we thank you... we thank you."

"That's not how it goes," said Lucy, angrily. She realized that Ruth was staring toward the doorway. Slowly, Mother, Father and Lucy looked up, too.

Standing in the door, with a heavy bag slung over her shoulder and another in her hand was a tall, dark figure. It was their long, lost aunt… Auntie Miriam.

Chapter 5

Uninvited Guest

Father and Mother had not seen Miriam in years. They almost didn't recognize her standing in their kitchen. She looked older, for sure. Her hair was a mess of black and grey curls as if she had blown here through the air. And there was a smell that followed her. A little bit sweet and a little bit… *garbagey*. However, her voice was just the same as Father remembered. It was a strong voice with a frosty chill.

"Well, I've been calling you all morning!" said Miriam, slumping her bags onto the kitchen floor. "Over and over. No answer."

Father stood up. There was a funny expression on his face. "Miriam! What a… surprise." He seemed to be searching for something else to say.

Luckily, Mother jumped in and took over. "It's very *nice* to see you after so long," she said, coming around the table towards Miriam. She placed a hand on the older lady's arm. "I'm afraid you've caught us on the day we try NOT to use our phones."

"Well, I don't care for phones either," said Miriam. "But this is an emergency."

Father quickly composed himself. "I'm sorry to hear that, Miriam," he said, placing an extra chair at the table. "Please sit down with us, if you'd like. We're just about to start breakfast."

"Well, I *am* starving," said Miriam. Without further delay she grabbed a bowl and spoon. "Oatmeal. Not my favorite, but I guess beggars can't be choosers."

Lucy became aware of something moving under the table. Her eyes grew wide. "You brought a kitty!" she said with delight. "Here, kitty-kitty."

The cat was licking at a drop of oatmeal under the table. It crouched down on the floor and leapt into Lucy's lap. The cat looked up at her with wide eyes.

"Oh, that's my cat, Frankie," said Miriam. "She's the social one in the family. The other cat, Johnny, is around here somewhere. Probably hiding."

"Frankie is a girl cat?" asked Lucy, tentatively petting the kitty. Frankie gave a sound that could have been a squeak or a purr. Lucy wasn't certain, but it almost sounded like the cat said a word. "Girrrl."

"Sure, she's a girl cat," said Miriam, noticing Lucy and Ruth for the first time. "And I suppose you are a little girl? And your brother, here… what's his name?"

"I'm Lucy," she said, proudly. "And this is my *sister*, Ruth. She has short hair but she's still a girl, too. We're *faternal* twins but we're both girls."

"FRATERNAL! It's fra-ter-nal," said Ruth. "Can't you ever get that right?" Mother raised her eyebrows, giving the girls a look that said *Don't even start.*

Miriam slurped down a big bite of oatmeal. And another. She turned toward Mother and Father. "Well, it has been a long time since we've seen each other. A long, bad time, actually. I lost my job at the library, and now I've lost my apartment, if you must know. It's this… cursed CITY. So I'm here to stay for a while, if you'll have me."

There was a noticeable silence. Father said, "Yes, of course we'll have you. You're family, sort of… I mean, yes. You're family, and we'll make up a room for you after breakfast."

With that, Frankie the cat settled into Lucy's lap, and they all resumed their breakfast. Miriam ate more oatmeal than they thought possible. Mother and Father got up to serve her second, third, fourth, and fifth helpings.

As she ate, Miriam seemed to be telling a story about everything that was bothering her. But it was hard to follow because she talked with her mouth full of oatmeal, and some dribbled down her chin. Still, Lucy and Ruth recognized a few words from her story: *rent, insurance,* some mean guy named *Pappa Doofus* or something? Most of all, she complained about "The Bay Area." Lucy guessed that's where Miriam used to live.

Finally, Miriam pushed her empty bowl back and wiped her chin. "Okay, that's better," she said. "Now, I'm tired. Let's see about these rooms."

Chapter 6

The House

Like many older Victorian houses, the Hoogablased's home *looked* very big and grand, with its huge windows and ornate facade. Inside, it was actually pretty small. On the first floor, there was a kitchen, living room and a small dining room. Upstairs were the bedrooms: one for Mother and Father, and a large, shared bedroom for the girls. They all had to share the upstairs bathroom. There was no extra space, unless you counted the super-cold basement, or the super-stuffed attic.

As Lucy cleared her breakfast bowl, a thought occurred to her. She reached over and tapped her sister's arm, whispering, "Where are they going to put Aunt Miriam? Like, where's she going to sleep?"

Ruth was still upset at her sister, and not in the mood to talk. But this point was too important to let go. "I don't know," Ruth whispered back. "But it better not be in our room. It's way too crowded already!"

Miriam was standing next to her bags, looking impatient. Father noticed and came around the table. "Well, Miriam. You must be tired. Let's take your bags upstairs and see what we can do."

"Oh, no!" thought Lucy. It was hard not to say it aloud, but inside

she was yelling, "Please don't put this strange woman in my room!"

Ruth was not able to keep her thoughts to herself. "Um... like, where is Aunt Miriam going to stay?"

A look passed across Father's face. "Well, Miriam is our guest, so let's take her bags upstairs and see where *she'd* like to stay."

Father grabbed the handle of Miriam's suitcase. His arm strained, and he bent his knees. The bag did not move off the floor. He chuckled a little, looking around at the rest of the family. He strained his arm again. The bag did not move. He tried lifting with both hands, with all his strength. The bag did not move. "What do you *have* in here, Miriam?"

Miriam sighed, moving toward her bag. "Well, pretty much everything I own in this lousy world," she said. She grabbed the handle, lifting the bag easily. She slung her other bag over her shoulder. "Come on, Frankie. Come on, Johnny, " she called over her shoulder. She walked quickly up the curved staircase.

Father and Mother were looking at each other. They didn't say anything, but the kids could tell what they were thinking. *What have we gotten ourselves into now?*

Chapter 7

Whose Bedroom?

Miriam quickly climbed the stairs and disappeared in the upstairs hallway. When the rest of the family found her, she was tapping on the hallway wall with the knuckle of her left hand. "As I suspected, this house has good bones."

"Bones? A house doesn't have bones," said Lucy, folding her arms across her chest.

"I think Auntie Miriam means the house has a solid foundation, kind of like having a good skeleton," said Mother.

"Skeleton?" asked Miriam, looking surprised. "Um, yes. Exactly." The older lady seemed kind of jumpy. "Now, I'll need a large space. I believe the girls' bedroom is the larger of the two?" She set off down the hallway.

Lucy and Ruth looked at each other. How did Miriam know theirs was the big bedroom? They followed their parents and Miriam down the hall, as if they were being marched off to a prison camp. "No way this is happening," whispered Ruth to her sister.

Lucy and Ruth's room was long and wide, with a bay window facing the back yard. As she stepped in, Miriam noticed a long piece of white tape running down the middle of the floor, all the way to the window. The line was fortified with several bookshelves, so it almost seemed like two separate rooms. "What's this?" asked Miriam, pointing to the tape. "The Maginot Line?"

The girls didn't know what she meant, but the tape was there for a reason. You see, the sisters had different tastes in almost everything. Their divided bedroom showed it, and the tape kept things nicely separated.

Ruth's style was what she called "Minimalism." Everything she had was black and white, or a shade of black, or a shade of white. Ruth's bed was an old army cot from a thrift store. Books lined the wall, and simple, dark clothing hung in her closet. Her only decoration was a framed black and white picture hanging on the wall. If it wasn't black

and white, Ruth said *no*.

Aunt Miriam puttered around, looking quizzically at her books. There was no time to lose, so Ruth sprang into action. "You know, Aunt Miriam, my side's really *not* very comfortable. It's dark. It's uncomfortable. Nothing soft to sit on, no extra space for books."

Miriam seemed to agree. She wandered toward the other side of the room.

Lucy's side was completely different. Lucy loved colorful posters of rainbows and unicorns. She had a bed with soft pillows, and bright clothing hung in her closet. Everything from the unicorn to the pillows to her clothes was a shade of just one color: pink. If it wasn't *pink, pink, pink,* then Lucy said *no, no, no.*

Lucy looked at Miriam, who was touring her side of the bedroom. "Aunt Miriam, you're welcome to stay on *my* side. But I don't think you'd like it too much. It's pretty girly, don't you think?"

"These children do TALK a lot," mumbled Miriam. "They're like chattering squirrels."

Before Lucy or Ruth could say anything more, Mother gave them a pleading look that said: *Please stay calm.*

Miriam was looking quizzically at Lucy's pink poster. Suddenly, she stepped back with a gasp. "Is that a… unicorn?"

"Yes, of course," answered Lucy. "I love unicorns. So cute and magical."

Miriam muttered under her breath. "Dreadful creatures!" Then she quickly turned away from Lucy's side. She heaved her bags onto the floor and sat down heavily on Ruth's cot.

"Well," said Father. "It seems Aunt Miriam has chosen Ruthie's bed for tonight, so maybe we'll set up a bed for Ruthie over by the window."

Ruth was so ready to complain. Why should she be the one to give up her place? Then she saw poor, old Miriam sitting on her cot, looking like she might fall asleep any moment. She decided she could stand it for a night or two.

Lucy was giggly with relief. She gestured toward the bay window, saying, "Oh, Ruth will *love* sleeping over there. She'll be right next to the guinea pigs!"

"The *what* pigs?" asked Miriam, suddenly coming awake. She stood up and walked towards the window. "You have pigs in here?"

"No, silly," said Lucy. "Our cute little *guinea pigs*. We each have one. Their names are Butterscotch and Ginsburg." She pointed to a cage at the window. Inside, two little animals, one with golden fur (Butterscotch), the other black and white (Ginsburg) were chewing nervously.

Miriam chuckled a little, which is the first time the family had heard her laugh. It was strange… a little like a laugh, a little like she was choking. Miriam moved closer to the cage. Lucy and Ruth followed her.

"It looks like my Frankie Cat has found some new friends!" said Miriam, chortling again.

"Oh my God!" yelled Lucy, rushing toward the cage. "No, Frankie! Don't hurt my Butterscotch!"

The cat was dangling her paw down into the cage, reaching for the terrified guinea pig. Her sharp claw was dangerously close to Butterscotch, who was shaking in fear. The guinea pig let out a *Squeeeeak!*

"Somebody do something!" shouted Lucy.

"Okay, okay," said Miriam. She picked Frankie up, cradling the cat in her arms. "Frankie's just playing around, giving your little rat a pat on the back. My cats are not going to *eat* your pets. They have better things to do."

"They better not!" shouted Lucy. She picked Butterscotch up, stroking his soft fur. She repeated herself, this time more quietly. "They better not."

———————————————————

It took a while to calm Lucy down. Mother hugged her and Father gave her a pat on the head. Mom also quietly checked the guinea pig cage, making sure the lid was secure. Ruth was also upset, but more about having to give up her bed. Finally, Mother made Miriam promise that she would keep an eye on the cats.

"Fine, fine," said Miriam. "Now, it's been a long day already. I'd like to get unpacked and rest."

Mother and Father offered to help her unpack. Miriam said she could manage it alone. As the family started to leave the bedroom, Miriam turned to the girls and said, "Thank you for sharing your room. I promise to be good." Miriam winked at them, which made Lucy feel a little better.

"Oh, and Hattie," she said to Mother. "I don't take lunch, but I'll want supper at 7:00 p.m. sharp. Maybe cook some meat this time?"

Mother was a bit taken aback. Was she supposed to cook for Miriam, like in a hotel or a restaurant? And there was another little problem. "Well, Miriam. I can cook, but we're vegetarians. We don't eat any meat."

"Okay, no worries," said Miriam. She fumbled around in her large bag. There seemed to be a lot of stuff in there. After a minute, she came to the door with something droopy and yellow in her hand. "You can cook this chicken. It's plucked and ready to go."

"Gross!" said Lucy.

"Ewww," said Ruth.

Mother didn't say anything, but her eyes were wide with alarm. Taking a handkerchief from her pocket, she delicately grabbed the chicken by the legs. Miriam chuckled once more. This time it was more like a belly laugh. "Don't

worry, dear. This bird won't bite. It's dead, dead, dead."

Father and Mother and the girls left the room, heading downstairs. Mother was carrying the chicken out in front of her. It was going to be a long day, indeed.

Chapter 8

Meat, Mum

It's never easy to have guests in your home. That's what Mom told Lucy, who was still upset. *But you should try to make any guest feel welcome.*

"I know, but who *is* she? I've never even met her," said Lucy as she made her way downstairs. Lucy was not so sure about these cats anymore, either... ever since the Butterscotch incident. When she reached the landing, she said, "And I wish her cats would stay outdoors."

Mom sighed, saying they'd have to be patient with *the situation.* Then she convinced Lucy and Ruth to resume their normal Saturday routine. Lucy set up her dollhouse in the living room, while Ruth read from a thick book. Father was doing some work, and Mother disappeared into the kitchen.

Upstairs, Miriam didn't seem to be resting at all. Every sort of clang, crack, and thud was coming from "her" room as she unpacked. All day long she was in the bedroom. As far as the family could tell, she didn't come out even once.

Around 6:30 in the evening, an unusual aroma wafted through the house. Lucy noticed it first. "Ewww. What is that smell?"

Ruth thought it smelled good, sort of Thanksgiving-y.

"That really smells delicious," said Father, coming down the stairs. Then he caught himself, realizing it was the smell of roasting chicken.

At 6:45 Miriam appeared in the kitchen. "I see the cats have found something they like," she said from the doorway. Frankie & Johnny were rolling on the floor in front of the oven, licking their lips and play fighting.

Mother dropped the peeler she was holding. "Oh. You startled me, Miriam."

"My dear," said Miriam. "I've brought you some special... herbs to cook along with that juicy bird?"

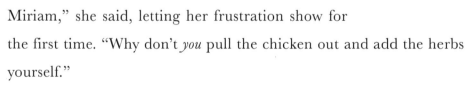

Mother did not enjoy cooking chicken or any other meat. She had been a vegetarian since she was about Ruth & Lucy's age, so touching and handling the chicken carcass was very unpleasant. "Well, Miriam," she said, letting her frustration show for the first time. "Why don't *you* pull the chicken out and add the herbs yourself."

"Fine, fine." She opened the oven door, pulling out the large roasting pan with her bare hands.

"Miriam!" yelled Mom. "Use some oven mitts, please. You'll burn your hands!"

"Fine, fine," said Miriam. She put on the mitts and stuffed a large pouch of strong-smelling herbs into the cavity of the bird. Frankie & Johnny were going absolutely crazy now, leaping and pawing. "Just a few more minutes, my pretties!"

At 7:00 the family gathered at the table. Mother had prepared yam curry and brown rice for the family. In the center of the table sat Miriam's big, golden brown chicken.

"Seems like you haven't had a good meal in ages," said Miriam, standing at the head of the table. Suddenly, she had a long, gleaming knife in her hand. Leaning over, she plunged the knife into the chicken. She expertly sliced the entire bird into breast pieces, wings, and legs. Before Mother could object, Frankie and Johnny each had a chicken leg to chew on.

Father was passing around the yams, but Lucy and Ruth weren't paying attention. They couldn't take their eyes off the chicken, with its crispy brown skin and sweet oozing juices.

Lucy found herself licking her lips just as she'd seen the cats do. "Mom," she whispered. "Can we please try the chicken?"

"Yeah, we've got to *try it*, Mom," said Ruth. "It's like having a real Thanksgiving meal for once!"

Mother had always said that if her children wanted to try meat, they should be free to choose. "Okay. But take it slow. Your stomach isn't used to it."

As soon as they had chicken on their plates, Lucy and Ruth were tearing into the juicy dark meat. It was the most delicious thing they'd ever tasted. Father and Mother had never seen them eat so ravenously, slurping and licking their fingers.

Lucy let out a huge burp. *Blaaaaaaarp.* "Oh, excuse me," she said, looking over at her mom. Mother was not amused.

"Very good. Very good!" said Miriam, smiling at Lucy. "No need to apologize for something natural!"

Miriam was eating an especially crunchy part of the bird. She gnawed, and crunched, and tore apart the meat with her teeth. "It's important to eat *all* of the bird," she said. "Out of respect for the animal."

"Wow, what's in that chicken, Miriam?" asked Father, smiling. He seemed like he wanted to see for himself, before it was all gone. Miriam quickly offered him a large piece, dropping it onto his plate with a flourish.

"It's an old recipe. The herbs and spices are… well, unusual," said Miriam, her mouth full of meat. She leaned her head back, opened her mouth, and bit into one of the chicken bones.

Lucy, Ruth and Father were focused on their meal. They were so busy they didn't notice that Miriam disappeared from the table and then reappeared.

"And what's a good dinner without a little entertainment?" said Miriam. She pulled a violin from its case, and held it under her chin. She steadied a long bow in her right hand, and started to saw it back and forth. A series of notes soared through the air: first fast and exciting, then slow and melancholy.

Father, Lucy and Ruth were entranced. They followed Miriam's swaying movements like cats following a mouse. Miriam looked *so* different from the tired woman they had seen in the morning. She seemed taller, and her hair was darker, shinier. *She really looks beautiful, like a Dark Queen from a story,* Ruth thought to herself.

To everyone's surprise, Father stood up and joined Miriam. He started to sing in a sweet voice as Miriam swooped and swayed with her violin. It went like this:

> *I set out running but I take my time*
> *A friend of the Devil is a friend of mine*
> *If I get home before daylight*
> *I just might get some sleep tonight*

Lucy & Ruth, who almost never got along, were following each other around the table. "Would you care to dance, Princess Lucinda," Ruth said to her sister, giggling.

"It would be my great honor, Count," replied Lucy with a straight face. Then they were giggling again. They tangoed around the table, Ruth spinning her sister. She had quickly drawn on a curly moustache with a magic marker.

When the music got slower, Ruth pulled Lucy close. In a foreign sounding accent she said, "D'you know that you are... my one true love." They were both laughing hysterically.

"I do know that," replied Lucy. She twirled her dress. "But fortunately, I am young and beautiful. Someday, I hope to do better!"

Now the girls could hardly stand up, they were laughing so hard. Miriam and Father continued to sing and play while the girls danced the night away.

Mother was still sitting quietly at her place. She was not a fan of loud music at the dinner table, even if this was one of Father's favorite tunes. As she sat, she folded her arms. Questions were forming in her mind: *Who was Miriam, after all? And what in the world had she put in that chicken?*

Chapter 9

Black Book

Everyone except Mother was in a rosy, good mood after dinner. Ruth and Lucy wanted to continue the fun.

"Well, it's not a school night, so I think it's all right," said Father. The girls were asking if they could stay up with their Auntie Miriam. "I'm bushed, myself. Thank you for an enchanting evening, Miriam."

"My pleasure," said Miriam, putting her violin in its case. "After all, we all have to sing for our supper now and again."

Father said he'd wash the dishes while Mom went up to bed. "I have a headache, but I'll be all right. Let's try to keep the noise down, okay?"

"I'm sorry if it was a little too loud," said Miriam. "Sometimes we get lost in the music, and the music takes away our troubles for a few minutes."

With that, Miriam led the girls upstairs. On entering their bedroom, Lucy and Ruth's jaws dropped. The room was completely transformed. The bookshelves were rearranged, and there seemed to be more of them. Each shelf was filled with musty old books, rolled up scrolls and maps, and lots of things the girls didn't recognize. The top of the bookshelf was crammed with bottles, jars full of slimy stuff, tweezers, seeds, dried leaves, and a flowering plant.

"Are you some kind of... scientist? Or something?" asked Lucy, examining the glass bottles. She picked up a jar with a big X on the label.

"Ah, ah, ah," said Miriam, taking the jar. "These things are delicate, and it's polite to ask permission. Some of these items are only for grown-ups, after all."

"Sorry," said Lucy, a little taken aback. After all it was *their* room, not Miriam's. She had totally reorganized without asking them.

Ruth was looking at the titles of the books. She pointed to the biggest, thickest, blackest book on the top shelf. "What's that one about?"

"That, my dears, is the Black Book, passed down to me from my mother, and her mother before her. And so forth." Miriam easily pulled the book from the shelf. "And after you put on your nightclothes, I will read from this very book."

"Nightclothes?" asked Lucy.

"*Nightclothes.* I like that," said Ruth. She turned to her sister. "I think Aunt Miriam means our pajamas."

Soon they were all ready. Miriam sat in an ornate rocking chair the girls had never seen before. They lounged on the rug, looking up at Miriam.

"What are you going to read?" asked Lucy.

"Ah, well," said Miriam. "I'm going to read you a poem. Actually, it's a very special poem that I wrote long ago...."

"YOU wrote a poem?" asked Lucy, her eyes wide. "So you're, like, a real writer?"

Ruth quickly jumped in. "What Lucy means is that we've never met an actual author, or poet, before."

Miriam smiled. After a pause, she said, "Well, almost anyone can write, no? But I'll let you be the judges if it's an *effective* poem or not."

Their aunt opened her Black Book. A cloud of dust spread out from the pages and glided throughout the room. Miriam found a page in the middle and pointed to a title, printed in large, curvy letters:

The Bellwether

"Bellwether? What does that mean?" asked Lucy. She was still skeptical about Aunt Miriam being an actual writer.

"Ah, ah," said Miriam. "It's best to listen and find out." With that, she began reading in a low, soothing voice:

Lying awake I toss and turn,

Navigating my bed's port and stern.

Oh, give me the tern 'twas born a bird.

She'll take me far away,

O'er mountain, lake, and on my merry way.

If only I could wish away my limbs' leaden aches...

To frolic in a land of candy and country cakes.

And as I lie awake, what is this vision I see?

No, really. What's this creature in front of me?

With a head of horns, glimmering eyes...

As she read, Lucy's eyelids began to flutter. She was having trouble keeping her eyes open. Ruth was also feeling sleepy, so she lay down on the rug. She propped up her head and tried to stay alert.

Miriam stopped and turned to the girls with a smile. "Maybe it's a little late for a poem? I see you are both getting very sleepy."

"No, we need to find out what that creature is," said Ruth. She started to yawn, and covered her mouth with her hand.

Lucy was already climbing into bed, pulling her soft, pink bedspread all the way up to her chin. "You can keep reading. I'll listen from bed."

"Maybe you'd *both* be more comfortable in bed," said Miriam. She quickly stood up, reached down and scooped Ruth up. "Let me tuck you into your comfy, little bed."

Before she could say anything, Ruth was transported across the room and inserted into her windowsill bed. Her aunt was remarkably strong for an old woman.

"Now, let's continue and see where this little poem takes us," said Miriam. She sat down in her armchair and reopened the Black Book.

With a head of horns, glimmering eyes

Its body shimmers, its nostrils flare,

And my little voice can't find its air.

Finally, I SHOUT. I shout again, and again.

The beast starts to low, for this is

How it speaks. And it starts to ring,

And thrash, and shuffle its feet.

This creature, at once so soft and pillow deep,

From nursery rhymes and a farmer's keep,

Is this what's become of my childhood friend,

The SHEEP?

And there's another, and another still.

They rumble and follow the herd.

What's heard is a low, monotonous meep.

As the bellwether leads... one sheep, two sheep,

three sheep...

And we who count, finally give ourselves up

To magical, irresistible,

Sleep, *sleep,* sleep.

Miriam looked over at Lucy, then Ruth. Both girls were fast asleep. The poem had done its work. She quietly closed the book and started to get up. Then she thought again. She opened the book and slammed it shut with a *Thwack*!

The girls slept on.

Miriam took a moment, looking around the large bedroom. Such a wonderful room, and much larger than the apartment she had abandoned this morning. It's a wonderful old house, she thought to herself. So full of promise and possibility.

Frankie and Johnny sidled up beside her in the chair. The cats were jumpy and expectant, their yellow eyes glimmering.

"So, my dears," said Miriam, waving her hand in the air. "Are you ready for the next phase?"

Johnny's little cat mouth opened. A creaky voice issued forth. "I am... I am ready."

Frankie's voice was louder and more confident. "WE ARE READY."

Miriam smiled at the cats. "Then let's begin. Frankie, you'll be lookout. Alert us if any of the family wake up. Johnny, you know what to do. And soon we'll have help."

In a flash, the cats scurried off on their missions.

And Miriam got to work.

Chapter 10

The
Seam

Miriam dug through a collection of things in her bag. She fished out a shiny object that turned out be an iron pot. She dug deeper. Then she had an old-fashioned quill pen. "Where is that thing?" she cried.

Finally, she had that wretched smartphone in her hand. With her big fingers, she punched at the screen. She waited. It was ringing.

"Biddy?" said Miriam into the phone. "Yes. YES. IT'S ME. We're in."

"In where? Where are you in?" asked the other person, sounding sleepy.

"IN THE HOUSE. The family's house," said Miriam, as loudly and clearly as she could. "You are to come right away. And call Ms. Snipwick!"

"Oh. Oh! Okay," said Biddy. "I had nearly forgotten."

"This could be the biggest thing since sliced bread, so DON'T FORGET!" said Miriam, slamming down the phone. She muttered to herself. "These old witches. It's a wonder you can get them out of bed in the evening!"

Miriam continued searching through her bag, assembling each item she found along the bedroom wall. "Oy! I need to get *organisized*," she said, chuckling to herself. Finally, she found what she was looking for: an old-fashioned stethoscope, the kind doctors use.

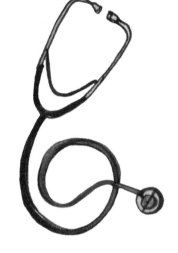

She approached the bedroom wall, between the door and bed on "Lucy's side" of the room. Her beloved Johnny cat was already pawing eagerly at the pink and gold wallpaper.

"Do you really think this is the place?" asked Miriam. With a nod from Johnny, she took up the stethoscope in her hands. She put the tips in her ears so she could hear. Then she moved the round bell of the stethoscope along the wall. As she moved it along, she listened. Now and then, she would rap on the wall with her knuckle, then listen even more attentively.

"Aaahaa! This just might be it." She leaned in for a closer listen.

"Well, good evening to you!" cried a voice from the far side of the room.

"Looks like you're on your way," said another person.

Miriam practically dropped her stethoscope. "Okay, okay," she said, taking it out of her ears. "No need to SHOUT."

The bedroom window was open, and cool air was rushing into the room. From the shadows two figures emerged: Ms. Entwistle, a largish

woman wearing colorful scarves, and a petite woman with spiky hair, Ms. Snipwick.

"Look at this posh house. Isn't this the cat's meow?" said Ms. Entwistle, looking around the bedroom and giggling.

"Are you sure the little princesses are asleep?" asked Ms. Snipwick, pointing to Lucy and Ruth in their beds.

"I read them the sleep poem. The long one. They should be out for a good, long while," said Miriam. Her eyes were gleaming.

Ms. Snipwick unbuttoned her cloak, and picked up the Black Book. "This old thing? Does it still work?"

Ms. Entwistle unwound her scarves. "Well, look at the sleeping beauties—I'd say the old book's still got some juice. Now let's get this party started." The jovial woman let out a nice, long belly laugh.

Miriam looked seriously at her friend. Then her look softened. "Yes, Biddy. We'll have some fun, for sure. And it's good to see you both. First things first, though... I *think* I've found the spot."

Miriam's old friends—and they were *old* friends, indeed—were surprised to hear she had gotten in so quickly. Sometimes it took months or years of study to find a house's *soft spot*. Of course, that depended on the house's age and history as well.

"Are you SURE this is an actual Darkhouse?" asked Ms. Snipwick, cautiously. "I don't remember reading about this location in Bierce, or any of the known literature."

"Well, the Council's made a mistake!" said Miriam, excitedly. "They didn't realize this is Chenery Street, formerly called *Warren Street*. Of course, you don't have to take my word for it."

Miriam wagged a finger in the air. She beckoned her friends close. She continued tapping on the wall, in nearly the same spot she had before.

"It's here somewhere," said Miriam. She put on the stethoscope again. There was hushed silence from the other ladies. *Rap-rap-rap. Tap. Tap. Tap.* Miriam searched the wall for just the right spot.

"Aaah!" Her eyes opened wide and she gave a delighted little scream. "This is it! We've got to mix up the portal potion, and fast."

Miriam quickly produced several small vials and specimen jars from her robe. She arranged them in a row on Ruth's nightstand, which she had taken for her own. She pointed to the glass bottles, one by one. "Here we have some home-grown herbs and spices: elixir of wormwood, and tincture of motherwort, dried lavender leaves, along with the pressed flowers of a witch hazel bush."

Miriam looked at her friends impatiently. "Well, have you brought what I asked?"

"I've got the rattlesnake venom," said Ms. Snipwick, proudly. "Not easy to come by, either." She placed a small vial among the others.

Ms. Entwistle looked a little nervous. She slowly brought out her contribution. "Well, ladies," she said. "I couldn't get the tears of a white dove. I tried and tried, but those doves are tough to catch!" She pointed to a little flask, containing a tiny amount of clear liquid. "I had to settle for pigeon tears."

"PIGEON?" shouted Miriam.

"Oh, Biddy," said Ms. Snipwick. "I just milked a rattlesnake for its venom, and you can't even catch a peaceful, little dove?"

"I happen to like doves very much," said Ms. Entwistle, defensively. "Honestly, I wouldn't *want* to see a dove cry."

"Okay, okay. I believe pigeon will do the trick," said Miriam. She was ready to get going. She picked up one flask, then another. Soon she was dancing back and forth mixing up the ingredients: a drop of snake venom here, a hint of wormwood there, a sprinkling of leaves and berries, and a sad pigeon's tears. All of it went into a small, iron pot.

Ms. Snipwick looked doubtfully at the little pot. "It's not exactly a big, black cauldron like in the stories."

"I know," said Miriam. "But this was so much *cheaper* than a full cauldron." She plugged in a hot plate, and set it as high as it would go. She placed the pot full of murky, greenish liquid on the burner. Soon the liquid started to swirl around. Then it began to bubble. Miriam stirred the concoction with a wooden spoon.

"Actually, this *is* like olden times," said Ms. Entwistle, cheerfully. "Like the stories my granny used to tell me."

When the frothy potion reached a rapid boil, Miriam took the pot off the little stove. "We'll see," she said, straining a little of the green liquid into a beaker.

She approached the wall, and carefully tipped the beaker. The greenish goo trickled out. There was a hissing, steaming sound as it made contact with the bedroom wall.

"Ha! Ha!" cried Miriam. "That's the sound! Like it says in the books, that's the sound we need."

Miriam moved her hand up and down the wall, smearing the green liquid. Up and down, up and down. As she rubbed, she created a long, green line. The more she rubbed, the softer the area got. It was as if the wallpaper and the wall beneath were melting away.

"This is the *seam*," said Miriam, her eyes glowing. "Now help me!"

Her friends joined in. They worked and worked at the wall.

Miriam's hand ached from so much activity. Still, she kept on. At last, her whole arm fell *into* the wall with a whooshing sound. She cocked her head to the side, looking back at her friends with relish. After years of hoping against hope, it was finally happening. "This is it."

"Wait, shouldn't we say something on this wonderful occasion?" asked Ms. Snipwick.

"What's there to say?" said Ms. Entwistle, snortling. "Let's do this, Witches."

One by one, the ladies gingerly stepped through the seam, into the wall and beyond.

Sunday School

Lucy awoke with a heavy sack on her head, or that's what it felt like. When she finally managed to open her eyes, the light was bright. Way too bright. It was later than usual. She sank back under her warm comforter with a whimper.

Ruth slowly sat up in her bed, groaning loudly. She was surprised to see Miriam still in her chair, in a dark corner of the room. Had she been sitting there all night? Her Black Book was open. Miriam was writing in it with an old-fashioned quill pen.

"What are you doing, Aunt Miriam?" asked Ruth, rubbing her eyes. "Geez, I had the weirdest dreams, and you...."

Before Miriam could answer, Mother appeared at their door. "Rise and shine, sleepyheads. It's already nine o'clock. Time to get ready for church!"

Ruth and Lucy both slumped back into their beds. It was Sunday, church day. While other kids were playing, they had to get dressed up and sit through a long church service AND Sunday school.

Ruth had an idea. She sat up again. "Maybe we could stay here this morning. With Miriam!"

Lucy nodded, adding, "Just this once, mom. After all, we have a guest!"

Mother seemed to think about it for a moment. "Well, maybe Miriam would like to join us at church?" She glanced at Miriam. The older lady was smiling. She looked like she might start laughing at any moment.

"Ha. Ha. No, that's fine. I'll stay here. My cats and I have some little things to do," said Miriam. And that was the end of the conversation, it seemed.

Lucy put on her nicest pink dress, with a little pink bow. Ruth chose dark leggings and a white button-down shirt. Ruth combed her short hair with a pick, and Lucy brushed out her long, blond hair.

"Hey, what's this?" asked Lucy, leaning down. She picked up a colorful pink and yellow scarf from the floor. "It's so pretty. Is it yours, Auntie Miriam?"

Miriam's eyes were wide with shock. She quickly composed herself. "Yes, of course. Why wouldn't it be?"

Lucy had an eye for fashion and color, and this was *not* something Miriam would wear. In fact, the old lady only seemed to own one or two purple coats, along with dark pants and big, clunky boots. After a pause, Lucy spoke up. "Do you think I could borrow the scarf sometime? If I promise to...."

"Fine, fine. No worries. You can take it now."

Lucy thanked Miriam, but her aunt didn't respond. She seemed preoccupied. Lucy wound the scarf around her petite neck, and she was ready to go. The girls said goodbye and headed to the door.

As she was leaving, Ruth saw something out of the corner of her eye. There was a thin, green line running down the length of the wall. As she watched, it became clearer. Was it a stain on the wallpaper she hadn't noticed before? But when she blinked her eyes the stain was gone. "My eyes must be playing tricks on me," she said to herself.

Father and Mother had breakfast ready. "We had better hurry," said Father. "Don't want to be late for Sunday school."

"Why doesn't Miriam go to church?" asked Lucy. She knew her parents might not answer, but she wanted to ask anyway.

"Well…" said Father. "It's kind of a long story."

"I bet it's because she's Jewish," said Ruth, who sometimes surprised the family by knowing things most nine-year-olds did not. "It's like Ruth Bader Ginsburg. She's Jewish too, and Jewish people worship on the Sabbath. That's Saturday, or technically starting Friday evening."

Ruth's favorite person in the whole world was Ruth Bader Ginsburg, a Justice on the Supreme Court. Ruth had written reports and dressed as RBG for Halloween. She even named her guinea pig Ginsburg. Ruth talked about her so much it drove Lucy crazy.

"Oh, please! Don't talk about Ruth Vader Whatever again! Anyway, how can Auntie Miriam be Jewish and we're *not* Jewish?"

"Because she's not related to us *by blood*," said Ruth, calmly. Then she added, "You dummy."

"You're the dummy, *dummy!*" said Lucy.

"Oh, nice one. Very original," said Ruth, rolling her eyes. "You *ignoramus*."

"Okay, girls. Okay," said Mom, looking severely at both of them. "Remember, we can disagree without being *disagreeable*, as Ms. Ginsburg herself has said."

"Anyway, Miriam was raised Catholic, not Jewish," said Father. It often seemed like he wasn't paying any attention, and then *snap!* surprised you with an answer.

Ruth thought this over. There was something missing in the information they were getting. "Okay, she's Catholic then. But why doesn't she have to go to church?"

Father looked up from his oatmeal. "Well, I guess it's because she's a grownup, and she can make her own decisions. Just like you will someday, though I hope you'll choose wisely."

"Not much chance of that!" said Lucy. Finally, she had scored a point against her sister.

Ruth was furious. She was reaching for her sister's face when

Mother intervened. "Enough!" She moved Lucy to one side of the table, and Ruth to the other. Mother sat in between to keep the peace.

Lucy couldn't quite let it go yet. She thought of another insult and aimed it at her sister. "Yeah, I bet Ruth Vader never had a sister like mine. One who thinks she's *so smart...*" said Lucy. Then she remembered what she really wanted to say. "I bet you're not even my sister. I bet you're adopted, or something!"

"You little witch. How dare you even say that!" Ruth stood up. She was ready to pounce on her sister.

"Girls!" shouted Mother, raising her hands. "We can't have any more of this, especially on Sunday, right before church services."

Mother tried another approach. She gave each girl a hug, saying, "I know it's confusing, but we can talk about that other stuff another time. Let's finish up so we can get going."

Actually, it wasn't confusing at all, thought Ruth. Their parents had simply refused to tell them much of anything. Which was typical.

As the girls finished their breakfasts, Father decided he would wait to tell them the rest of Miriam's story: how she had been married to his brother Jack, gotten divorced, been homeless for a while, and so on.... it was all just a little too much for this morning.

After breakfast, they made their final preparations for church. As she was putting on her coat, Ruth said under her breath. "By the way, Ruth Bader Ginsburg *did* have a sister. And I bet she was really smart and *nice.*"

Chapter 12

Rodents
Revisited

It was a beautiful spring day. Sunny. No sign of fog. Of course, Ruth and Lucy had to spend most of the morning inside a dark church. Afterwards, Mother and Father offered to take them to their favorite brunch spot: *Toast*. They didn't mind waiting for a table because the weather was so nice.

As they stood in line, Mother pointed to the fresh breads in the window. "Wow, look at all of the choices. What are we going to have?"

They finally sat down and opened their menus. Mother seemed very excited. "Look. They have seven-grain bread, homemade sourdough, double and even triple wheat with extra spelt. Lucy—there's one here called Unicorn Sweet Bread, and it's gluten-free!"

"Um, mom?" said Lucy, batting her eyelashes a little.

"Yes?" Mother looked a little nervous, as if she knew what was coming.

"I know you love toast. But I'm thinking of getting something different this time. Eggs. Over easy! And gluten-free pancakes."

"Okay, that's fine." Mother looked a little relieved.

Ruth put down her menu. "I'm getting eggs, too. And I see you can get bacon for an extra $3.00. That sounds perfect."

Mother looked queasy. "Oh, my, is this how it's going to be?" She sighed. "Well, if you really want to eat charred animal flesh. It's your choice."

So Ruth added bacon to her order, extra juicy. She shared a piece with Lucy during the meal. "Thank you, Count," said Lucy, smiling at her sister. "You're always a gentleman."

Ruth smiled back. Maybe this day would turn out okay, after all.

After brunch, the family packed into their little car and headed home. "I wonder what Miriam's been doing all this time?" asked Lucy.

Her parents wondered, too.

———————————

They arrived home but didn't see Miriam anywhere. Father and

Mother went upstairs to change into "casual clothes." The girls decided not to change just yet. Ruth picked up her book, and Lucy wandered toward the kitchen.

"Aaaaaah!" Lucy was screaming from behind the kitchen door.

"What is it now?" said Ruth, putting down her book. She swung open the kitchen door and saw Lucy bent over something. She moved in to get a better view.

"Aaaaaah!" Now Ruth was screaming. "Is that Butterscotch?"

"Let go of my Butterscotch you horrible cat!" screamed Lucy. Now she was kicking and flailing her arms at Frankie. In the cat's mouth, gripped in her teeth was a golden, quivering ball of fur.

"What's going on?" said Mother, rushing into the kitchen. She moved toward Lucy and the cat. Now Mother was kicking at the cat. "Drop that poor creature this instant!" she yelled at Frankie, as if the cat could understand. The cat didn't listen; she actually seemed to be smiling as she gnawed the furry creature.

"What's all the commotion?" said a voice from outside the back door. Coming in, Miriam looked at the scene. She leaned down and gave Frankie a little pat on the head. "My dear, what have you got there? A little friend?"

Miriam had a pair of garden scissors in her hand. Before anyone could move, she took the fur ball from

Frankie's mouth. With her other hand, she plunged the sharp scissors deep into the furry animal. It made a little whimper and died. "Well, we couldn't let the poor thing suffer," she explained.

"YOU NASTY OLD WITCH!" said Lucy. "I HATE YOU. AND YOUR CATS!"

"My, oh my," said Miriam. She was remarkably calm. "I can see you're upset. Really, you shouldn't be. You see, this is NOT one of your little pet rats. It's just a garden variety *gopher*."

Miriam threw the dead gopher back to her cat, who was delighted to keep pawing at it. "You see, we've been out in that so-called 'garden' of yours. It's infested with gophers; little wonder nothing will grow!"

The family was in shock. Lucy was sobbing, and her mother put an arm around her. Mother turned to Miriam. "Please get that cat and that poor, dead animal out of this house at once!"

"Fine, fine," said Miriam. She strolled to the back door, opening it. Frankie obediently took her fresh kill outdoors. "I wonder if you wouldn't join me in the back yard for a minute. If you're willing to follow an 'old witch' that is…"

Reluctantly, Mother and her girls followed Miriam out onto the back porch. Miriam was pointing down at the ground. Underneath the stairs was a huge pile of fur and tails, a mound of dead gophers killed by the cats. It did not smell good.

Miriam was waving her garden clippers in the air. There was gopher blood on them, too. "Well, you see what we've had to deal with…"

"What IS all this? It's just so GROSS!" said Lucy. She moved closer

to her Mother, in case she needed to hide her eyes.

"Sorry to be the bearer of shocking news," said Miriam. "But did you ever wonder why nothing would grow in this garden?" She waved her hand toward the long mound of dirt and dead plants. "Well, it's because these gophers were eating up your plants—roots, stems, and everything. And now, my little cats have taken care of the problem, once and for all."

It was a shock to see all of those furry little animals in a pile, to be sure. But mother had to admit she was happy to have the gophers gone. Miriam offered to clean it all up. She said she might be able to do something with the garden, as well. "You'll see, in the end it'll be all right," said Miriam.

"Okay, I guess so," said Lucy, after her mother had explained again about the gophers. "But those cats better stay away from my Butterscotch. And Ginsburg, too."

Mother and the girls were ready to go inside. As they opened the back door, Father appeared, smiling. He had put on his colorful beach shorts. "So, how's everybody doing? Beautiful day, huh?"

That's the thing about fathers—they can be totally clueless, like they're not paying any attention at all.

If the Hoogablased family had a motto it was this: Weekends are for relaxing (and church), but weekdays are for work, work, and more work. Harry and Hattie Hoogablased rose at six o'clock Monday morning ready to go. Ruth and Lucy were expected to be up by 6:30, even though school didn't begin until 8:40.

Harry and Hattie had started their own company at the beginning of the year. It was called *Goober.com.* So far, Goober was a big success. Their main business was helping schools identify kids with nut allergies, and business was booming. It seemed everyone in the city had one allergy or another. Mother and Father were busy from early morning into the night.

This Monday was a particularly exciting day for Goober. The company sign was finally arriving by Priority Overnight mail. Harry bounded down the stairs when he heard the doorbell ring at 6:05. It was their UPS man, Big Mike, with a huge package.

"Mike, so glad to see ya," said Harry, opening the front door. "Come in."

"This is a big one, Harry," said Mike. He was a large guy, easily two hundred and fifty pounds. Still, he had to use all his strength to lift the package up the front steps. Now he was winded. "Have to admit, the back's hurting a little on this one."

"Let me help you!" said Harry, grabbing at the package in the doorway. They both strained and stretched trying to pull it into the house.

"Oh, hey," said Mike, dropping the package. "I see you have a... houseguest?"

"Yes, hello," said Miriam, who had silently appeared in the doorway. "A little early for all this ruckus, no?" Miriam picked up the long package with one hand, easily tucking it under her arm. She placed the package on a table, and cut it open with a little knife. She seemed to have every sort of knife at hand whenever she needed it.

"Wow, okay," said Mike, giving Harry a look. "I'd better be on my way." He gave Harry a fist bump before leaving. "Um, nice to meet you," he called back through the doorway, in Miriam's direction.

"Fine, fine," replied Miriam.

Slowly the whole family gathered in the living room. Lucy and Ruth were up even earlier than usual. Ruth was rubbing the sleep from her eyes. When she saw the sign, her eyes opened wide.

Before them on the table, was a giant peanut shape with the letters GOOBER.com in bubble letters.

Miriam tried to resist, but couldn't hold back. She started with a snicker, which grew into a low chortle, which grew into a belly laugh. "Ha, ha, ha! This is the great startup, the one that's making you rich? A company called GOOBER?"

Ruth and Lucy were laughing a little, too. Goober sounded like something gross, like snot or boogers. That's what kids at school said, too.

Hattie tried to explain that lots of startup companies had funny names. There was Uber for riding, Twitter for twitting, Womber for baby monitoring, and Google for googling anything else you needed. So, why not Goober?

"And Goober for *goobing*," whispered Lucy. Then she and Ruth were laughing.

"And they think I'm strange," said Miriam offhandedly. The older lady had seen several booms and busts in the city, which always brought out the most ridiculous company ideas. Still it made her titter.

Father's face turned bright red. Until now, he had kept his cool with Miriam, even when she was annoying. Suddenly he burst forth. "GOOBER is the business that keeps a roof over our heads. OUR heads, mine and yours, I might remind you, Miriam."

Miriam apologized for laughing. It had been a long week and she needed a good chuckle. At Mother and Father's request, she helped them install the sign above a side door on the house. She also agreed to help out the family during the busy weekdays. "Just wait and see what I do with that sad, little garden," said Miriam. "It'll be so nice, before long you'll want to pay me."

As Father and Mother had found out, Miriam could be difficult. Still, they were trying to be optimistic. And if she could do anything with that garden, it would be nothing short of a miracle. At least it would keep her busy.

Chapter 13

The Village Gardener

Miriam turned out to be quite a gardener. While Mother and Father worked upstairs and the girls were at school, Miriam was out in the garden. First, she dug up the entire plot from the house to the tree stump near the back fence. She hoed the soil. She tilled the soil. She planted seeds and watered them. All the while, Frankie & Johnny were at her side. There would be no more pesky garden gophers, that's for sure.

In a day or so, seedlings sprouted and sent out green leaves. A week later, they were small healthy plants. Several weeks after that, the garden was a rich tangle of vines and exotic plants.

Mother and Father were so busy they barely noticed. Ruth and Lucy noticed it, though. So did their friends from school. The plants were so tall and eye-catching they could be seen from the street. And they had sprung up so *fast*.

Ruth offered to help with the garden, so Miriam gladly put her to work. "The main thing plants need are love & talking to," said Miriam. She led Ruth through the garden, pointing out plants and calling each one by name. "This is Hortense, a beautiful passionflower vine. How are you today, Hortense?"

The vine seemed to move slightly, as if it were answering.

Miriam led Ruth deeper into the garden. It was so dark and overgrown that Ruth could barely see the sky above. Ruth pointed to a colorful shrubbery, saying, "What's this one called?"

"Not what, but *who*!" said Miriam. "This is Mattie, our very own motherwort herb. Why don't you pick a couple of her leaves? We'll make a tea to calm your mother's nerves."

"Oh, is that why it's called Motherwort?" asked Ruth. "Because it's for mothers, or something? Does it cure warts, too?"

Miriam gave a nice, hearty laugh. "That's a good one. I'll have to remember it." But she didn't say anything more.

Ruth carefully approached the Motherwort plant. As she picked its dark green leaves, the plant seemed to quiver slightly. It wasn't an unhappy quiver, more of a friendly shake. She would swear the plant was almost dancing in place.

"Now, let me show you a little trick," said Miriam, winking at Ruth.

"But it's a secret. Can you handle a *secret?*"

Now Ruth was really interested. Was Miriam going to shed some light on why she was… well, so odd? Ruth scanned back over the last couple of days, thinking about her aunt. She seemed to know everything about the family and their house. And whenever her name was spoken, Miriam suddenly appeared out of nowhere, almost as if she could hear and see everything, everywhere. *Oh, and then there's this garden,* thought Ruth.

Miriam smiled, putting her arm gently on Ruth's shoulder. "I think you and I are more alike than you know," she began. "We see things others don't see. We know things others might not know?"

Ruth was quiet. She wasn't so sure about this.

Aunt Miriam nodded. "Think about it, and I believe you'll understand. Now, I have something to show you." The older lady wrapped a finger under the leaf of a fig tree. She started to make a low, murmuring sound. Then it became a buzzing sound, as if there were a huge swarm of insects buzzing around underground, under their feet. Without even moving her lips, Miriam continued the sound:

Bbbbbbbbbbbuuuuuuuuuuuuuzzzzzzzzzuuuummmmmm

Before their eyes, bees began to gather. It started with a few stray honeybees. Soon they were joined by big, yellow bumblebees. Then the fattest, furriest bees slowly came in.

A smile played across Miriam's face. "Would you like to try? I think you could do it, if you tried."

Ruth had a sudden feeling of confidence. Stepping up, she wrapped her little finger around a leaf, as she had seen Miriam do.

"That's right," said Miriam. "Keep going."

Then Ruth started to hum. Her voice sounded different, more resonant. *Bbbbbbbuuuuuuuuuuuuzzzzzzz.*

A single bee flew in and landed on Ruth's arm. It started to crawl through her little arm hairs. Ruth was frozen still as a statue. Had she summoned this bee?

"Not to worry, my dear," said Miriam. "These are our friends." She casually waved her finger in the air. The fat bee crawled a couple more steps up Ruth's arm and took off.

"That's amazing," whispered Ruth. "How did you do that? And how did I do that?"

Miriam was smiling. "Ah, ah, ah. Not yet. All will be revealed in good time, but remember: It's a SECRET. It's not to be told to your dear mother, sister, teacher, preacher, or your best friend."

"Oh. I don't really have a best friend, anyway," replied Ruth. "Most of the kids in my class are kind of lame. And they all like Lucy better, anyway."

"I understand," said Miriam. "It's been the same for me. We're a little different. And other people have trouble dealing with that."

"Um. Yeah, I guess so." Ruth wondered why Miriam had chosen to share all of these things with her.

Miriam led Ruth further down the garden path. The swarm of bees spread out in organized groups around Miriam. "Now, let's follow the bees, and watch them do their magic." She held aside the leaves of a large, dark plant so they could pass.

Slowly Ruth realized that the entire garden was buzzing and wriggling. Everywhere she looked a fat bee was dragging its abdomen over a flowering plant. Here and there, sparrows were swooping down to pick off a stray bee. And there were larger birds up in the tree branches making strange noises.

"Wait," said Ruth, hurrying down the path. "We have a tree now?" She reached the place where the tree stump had been. In its place was a huge tree with silver bark and leafy boughs. She reached out to it. The tree seemed to reach back, extending its green leaves to greet her.

"This is Marjorie," said Miriam, giving a little bow to the silver tree. "She just needed a little attention. With a little luck, in a few months she'll be back to her full height. Almost like it was 1968 all over again."

"Um, wow," said Ruth. Some of the things her aunt said were *pretty out there*.

"Now remember, my dear," said Miriam. "For now, all of this is between us."

Ruth nodded quietly. Of course, she wanted to tell her sister, her mother, and the rest of the world. What would her teacher, Mr. Tembruell, think of all this? *Anyway, I guess I've made a promise,* Ruth said to herself. She hoped she could keep it.

The pair continued their work in the garden. They spent hours tending and talking to the plants.

Lucy wasn't all that interested in gardening. She was busy with school and play-dates. Her second best friend, Amelia, had seen

Miriam through the open gate one morning and asked, "Who is that lady? Does she live with you?"

Lucy's cheeks flushed red. "Oh. She's just doing some work for us." Later, she felt bad about it. But she was also a little embarrassed by her aunt.

Up and down Chenery street, neighbors were commenting on the new garden and the mysterious gardener as they peeked through holes in the fence. "It's just amazing!" said their next-door neighbor, Ms. Sanchez. Rhoda the crossing guard said she'd never seen anything like it. As usual, Big Mike the UPS man had more information than the rest. "It's that houseguest staying with the Hoogablaseds. You know, the tall woman with dark hair? Her name's Miriam Levin and there's something unusual about her, kind of mysterious."

Several weeks had passed since Miriam had come to the Hoogablased home. In all that time, Miriam had not left the house—a fact that Father and Mother were apparently too busy to notice.

Miriam never even ventured out onto the sidewalk, she was so concerned about her privacy. When she saw little eyes and noses peeping through holes in the fence, she got terribly angry. She poked at those eyes with the handle of her broom. "Mind your own business, nosy neighbors. Shoo! Shoo!"

Chapter 14

Dumbwaiter

Ruth and Miriam were becoming close companions: hanging out in the garden, talking late into the night, reading the same books. Ruth was starting to dress like her aunt in a long, dark cloak from her favorite thrift store. Her hair seemed darker and wavier as well.

As usual, Lucy was the first to comment. One evening as Ruth and Miriam worked side by side in the kitchen, Lucy whispered to her Mother. "Ruthie looks really weird, don't you think? I mean, she's like, totally gone GOTH overnight. Is all this stuff *okay* with you?"

Mother considered for a moment. "Well, I don't like the dark mascara. But overall, I think she looks pretty good. And I'm glad she's getting along so well with her aunt. Maybe you could take a page from your sister, on that score?"

"No way!" said Lucy, furrowing her brow. "I'm not going over to the dark side, no matter what anyone says."

Mother chuckled a little. She had learned to mostly stay on the sidelines when it came to the girls' fashion choices. "Well, maybe you could at least help your sister in the kitchen."

Miriam and Ruth had a surprise. They were cooking an elaborate dinner: beef brisket and roasted parsnips, with a special vegetable stew just for Mother. As usual, Miriam supplied a special packet of garden herbs that made everything super yummy. Mother was pleased. Father was away on a business trip to Sacramento, so she would take any help she could get.

They decided to dine at the kitchen table. They all ate heartily. Ruth and Lucy were licking their lips as they dug into the brisket. After dinner, they offered to help clean up the dishes.

"Well, this is quite a treat," said Mother. She leaned back in her chair.

"You just sit right there, Hattie. We've got this." Miriam rinsed, and Ruth loaded the dishes into the dishwasher. Lucy joined in, drying the pans and roasting rack. Soon they had an efficient machine going and Miriam was humming a tune.

As she reached a crescendo in the song, there was a loud rattling sound. It was coming from somewhere in the kitchen.

"Oh my gosh. The dumbwaiter thingy is moving," shouted Lucy, pointing to the old contraption in the wall.

"No, no," said Mother. "That's impossible. That thing hasn't worked in years."

And yet, the rattling continued. The dumbwaiter was creaking back to life. They could hear the wheel spinning and the rope moving.

The dumbwaiter came to a stop with a thud. Yellow eyes appeared out of the darkness. Those eyes look familiar, thought Lucy.

"Ah ha! My dears," said Miriam, approaching her cats. "I see you've found a new place to play." She picked up Frankie and Johnny in her broad arms.

Mother's surprised look lingered for a while. She seemed to be thinking, but kept her thoughts to herself. Finally she spoke up. "Will wonders never cease? When we bought this house, we were told the dumbwaiter wasn't even hooked up. It was only for show."

"Ah, well. This house has a long and rich history," said Miriam, addressing the whole family. "Did you know that the house was built in 1889? And several prominent families have lived here throughout the...."

Lucy and Ruth weren't interested in a history lesson. They wanted to try out the dumbwaiter right away. Ruth turned to her sister. "Excuse me, but are *you* the dumb waiter?"

"Yes, I am. But surely YOU are the dumber waiter," said Lucy, not missing a beat.

"But certainly you are the dumbest waiter of them all!"

They were laughing as they loaded up several heavy cookbooks on the wooden tray of the old dumbwaiter. Then Ruth grabbed the rope, and started to pull. There was a *creeeeak*. It didn't budge. She pulled again. Nothing.

"Ah, these old things need a little elbow grease," explained Miriam. She grabbed the rope and spun it through her hands. The cookbooks went upwards into the house and disappeared.

"But where did it go?" asked Lucy. She was actually a little bit stumped. She didn't remember seeing any kind of opening or panel upstairs.

"Oh, we'll find it," said Miriam. "If it goes up, it must be *somewhere*."

Mother let out a yawn, then covered her mouth. "I'm sorry, girls. I'm beat. Better head up to bed. Miriam, thank you for a wonderful dinner. Do you think you might get the girls...?" Mother yawned again, mid-sentence. "Excuse me. Could you put the girls to bed?"

Miriam said it would be her pleasure. She might even read her new poem aloud, if the girls consented.

"Sure, that'd be great," said Ruth.

"Wait, what?" said Lucy. She was not in the mood for another of Miriam's so-called poems. She tried to think of an excuse, but came up short. "I'm kind of tired, but I guess I could listen a little. Now let's find those cookbooks!"

Miriam took the girls upstairs after Mother had said goodnight.

On entering the girls' bedroom, Miriam quickly opened a small panel in the bedroom wall. She pulled out the cookbooks, good as new. She closed the panel as quickly as she'd opened it.

"I wanted to look down there," said Lucy, a whiney tone in her voice. "I mean, I've never even seen that little door in our room. Has it been here all along?"

Miriam put an arm around Lucy's shoulder. "All in good time," she said. "Now it's getting late and I promised an early bed-time and a poem."

Actually, she had promised no such thing, thought Lucy. She looked over at Ruth, who was quietly putting on her *nightclothes*. It seemed to Lucy that her sister was completely under the spell of their old aunt. And it annoyed her.

Miriam pulled her Black Book from its place on the shelf. She had taken over most of what was formerly Ruth's part of the room. Ruth sat on the rug. Lucy decided to curl up in bed. "I can hear perfectly well from here."

Miriam started with an introduction. "Well, I've been writing little poems for many, many years in many different... circumstances. Tonight I'm going to read a new one composed right here in this lovely home."

Ruth was paying attention, but stifling a yawn. She was determined to stay alert to the end.

Lucy, on the other hand, was wide awake. She did not intend to listen to another silly poem. Instead, she had a graphic novel partly hidden under the covers so she could read about something more interesting: *Eunice the Unicorn.*

Miriam cleared her throat. "Ahem, as I said, this is a new poem. It is dedicated to the Hoogablased household." She turned to a new page in the book, and began reading in a surprisingly sweet voice.

The House

A darkened house, long abandoned
By spirits and the memories of men
Comes back to life,
At the drop of a pin.

Wait, what's that?
Is it only the wind, or a scurrying rat?
Suddenly, there's a flicker from within
This hollow body is alive again.

A verdant garden grows,
This home is full of light,
Mystery and magick comingle under
The quiet care of night....

Miriam had read barely half of the poem when she closed the book. Neither of the girls said a word. She tiptoed over to check. As she pulled back the covers for a peek, Ruth let out a long snore. Good, she was sound asleep. Miriam made her way to Lucy's bed. Her little eyelashes were shut tight. There was no sound beyond her regular breathing.

Clap! Miriam clapped her hands together, but Lucy didn't stir. She must be asleep.

Miriam let out a long sigh. It took a lot of effort to get a quiet moment in this house. And she needed every minute if she was going to bring a real *Darkhouse* back to life. She quickly found her phone and made a call.

"I think I left a scarf here!" said Ms. Entwistle, squeezing her large frame through the window. She had plenty of other scarves wrapped tightly around her neck.

"You're *always* leaving things," said Ms. Snipwick.

Miriam beamed a nice, big pleasant smile. For once, she did not look tired or annoyed or out of sorts. She looked positively radiant, as if she had discovered a fountain of everlasting youth.

"It's really happening," Miriam said quietly. "Like those old stories where a Witch lives in an enchanted house? Well, now WE are those witches, and THIS is our house! I'm already feeding on its power."

"Really? That seems a bit sudden," said Ms. Snipwick, suspiciously. "Is it safe? We should really alert the Council...."

"Oh, you worry too much!" said Miriam. She grabbed her friends' hands for a demonstration. She chanted in a low voice, and the bedroom walls began to glow.

"Oh, I see," said Ms. Snipwick.

"Lady, you are on fire!" said Ms. Entwistle.

A powerful light emanated from the walls. Ms. Entwistle and Ms. Snipwick looked around curiously, partly shielding their eyes against the brightness. Then they heard a sound, like giant ants creeping through a dry forest. Little, green vines poked their leaves out of the base of the wall. They got bigger and livelier. The vines were creeping up the walls before their eyes. Soon the vines were encircling their legs, and coiling up their backs.

"Oh, my. That tickles!" said Ms. Entwistle.

The vines climbed higher, and spread their leaves. The bedroom was swimming in a sea of passionflower, honeysuckle, and Virginia creeper vines. A lovely fragrance traveled through the air as bright flowers opened up.

Ms. Entwistle was doing the backstroke through the green creepers, trying to find some room to breathe.

Ms. Snipwick was so tightly wrapped in vines, her glasses were on the verge of falling off. "Okay, Miriam. It's wonderful, we get it," she said, pushing back against giant green leaves. "That's quite enough for now!"

"Fine, fine," said Miriam. She let the vines creep along the ceiling, then she bowed her head. The glittering light went out, and the vines crept back down. They were gone as soon as they had come.

"That's just a little taste of what's here, harkening back to days past, forty years ago, when vines covered these walls."

"Wow. Just amazing," said Ms. Entwistle.

Ms. Snipwick, who always tried to keep an even keel, said, "Yes, it's quite impressive. Now, I see that the princesses sleep tonight, perchance to dream. And for us, it's time for the *seam*."

The ladies laughed and danced through the room in a mini-conga line. They hadn't had this much fun in years. Miriam made the lights flash again, as they gathered around the little cookstove.

"Time to brew up a fresh potion," said Miriam. "What have you brought me?"

The ladies poured their mysterious ingredients into the iron pot, as they had before: herbs from the garden and other little treats.

"This time, I have fresh venom from a black widow spider," said Sally Snipwick, who specialized in poisonous secretions.

"And I have real crocodile tears!" said Biddy Entwistle, pulling a jar from her coat pocket. "I can tell you, the crocs at the zoo are real bawlers, especially when you pull their tails."

It was an impressive array of ingredients that Miriam boiled into a thick, murky stew. Then she applied it to the wall, as before. The seam opened up like a dream. And just like that, they were ready to go.

Before they went beyond, Miriam gave a quick glance at Lucy and Ruth. They were sleeping soundly in their beds. Neither one had made a peep.

"Oh, my God!" whispered Lucy to herself. "What are they doing now?" She wasn't sure if she was asleep or awake. She remembered reading her comic under the covers. Then she had dozed off. She saw unicorns in a bright field munching on tangled, green vines. Later she heard voices and she could see her own bedroom, but it looked different.

There was a strange cooking smell wafting through the room. Lucy opened her eyes. There was Miriam, along with two other dark figures. Bright light was pouring into the room through a gap in the wall. The ladies—if they were ladies—were buzzing like bees around the gap. They reached their long arms toward the light.

Lucy had to stifle a scream. She forced her mouth shut but kept her eyes wide open. If this was a dream, she hoped it would be over soon. If this was real life, she *had to* stay quiet.

Miriam and the other ladies were entering the gap. As they did, a brief flash of light overtook them. Lucy heard a cry of delight. Then the bedroom was dark again.

Chapter 15

Wide
Awake

Lucy spent what seemed like an hour peering out from under her comforter, eyes trained on the wall. Minute after minute ticked by. Nothing changed.

She was thinking about their house. What was behind their bedroom wall? Was it the hallway, or the bathroom? There were only three rooms upstairs: her bedroom, the bathroom, and her parents' room. Of course, there were a few closets but where could anyone go? Then again, you could never tell with dreams. A house could definitely expand if you were having a nightmare. You could find new rooms, or wander into a totally different place.

Well, Lucy couldn't go back to sleep, and she couldn't keep staring at a wall. If this *was* a dream, why was she lying in bed? She wanted to float around or something, not just shiver under the covers. So she pulled back her comforter as quietly as she could. She swung her left leg out and put a single toe on the fuzzy, pink rug. So far, so good. She could feel the ground under the rug. It was solid.

She tiptoed through the dark bedroom toward the wall. As she made her way, she heard Ruthie snoring away from her little bed in the alcove. Maybe she should wake her sister. Then again, this could all be a....

Whoa! Lucy bumped into the wall. It came sooner than she expected. She rubbed her hand side to side, feeling for where the big gap was. She searched, but it was no longer there.

Just then, she heard laughter. It was coming from *inside* the wall. She knew that laugh—it was Miriam's. "That's where they've gone!" Lucy cried out, pointing at the wall. As the laughter continued, she tried to follow it, or find its source.

She stumbled out of the bedroom, into the hallway. It wasn't dark, and it wasn't light either. She was walking through a purple haze. She pressed her back against the hallway wall and let it guide her forward. She took a step, then another. Wait, she was curving back to where she started. Now she was back at her bedroom door again!

"Mom! Where's my mom?" Lucy shouted, but no one answered. She had to get to Mother, straight away. She stepped firmly into the middle of the hallway, heading where she

thought her parents' room must be. She could feel the carpet under her feet. She tiptoed sideways down the hall, staying away from the walls. After more than a minute, she still hadn't even reached the bathroom. If she could only get there, she could flip on the light switch.

Boom! She ran right into a wall, banging her elbow. She gripped her arm. But there shouldn't be a wall here. She would swear that the House was turning against her, preventing her from reaching her parents' room. She lurched forward toward the nearest thing she could find. Again, it was the hallway wall. Reaching her hands out, she could tell there were wooden frames hanging there, something she didn't remember at all. As she peered upwards, she could see they were paintings in ornate, gold frames. Painted figures looked down from the pictures, their eyes

following her. One was an old man with beady eyes and a cane. The other painting was a beautiful woman, her arm around a golden-haired child. The eyes were captivating.

Almost against her will, she leaned in to see the woman and child. As she did, she realized the child looked remarkably like HER. It looked like her blonde hair, her eyes, and her freckles. And the little girl wore pink, though it was an old-fashioned kind of blouse Lucy would never wear.

"Aah!" Lucy let out a scream, then started to run up the hallway towards Mother's room. She ran and ran, as well as she could, down the long hallway. Finally she reached Mother and Father's large bedroom door.

She reached for the door handle. It felt warm. She turned it, and pushed open the door. As she did, bright light flooded the hallway. Lucy slowly put her hand towards her mouth. Her eyes grew wide as she stared into the most beautiful, bright, fiery light....

Then she screamed for real: a high, piercing wail.

"Maaaaamaaaa!"

Chapter 16

Soft Spot

"Lucy! Wake up, dear," said Mother, cradling her daughter in her arms. She applied a cold washcloth to Lucy's forehead. Her face was flushed and red.

Lucy screamed again. "Maama!" Then she woke with a start. Her big, blue eyes looked searchingly around the room. There was her mother, at last. Ruth was nearby, holding another washcloth in case it was needed. And she was back in her own bed, in her own bedroom.

"You gave us a scare," said Mother. She stroked Lucy's long hair.

"Oh, my God," said Lucy. "I'm so glad to be here." She sat up quickly, looking around the bedroom. "Wait, where's MIRIAM?"

The girls were not allowed to say *Oh my God!* However, Mother overlooked it this time. She leaned down and said quietly, "Well, Miriam's downstairs feeding her cats, I believe."

Lucy was confused. That stuff that happened last night—and she could see the light streaming in the window so it must be morning—well, it seemed *so real.* And if it was real, she HAD to tell Mother.

"Have you noticed anything… like, *totally strange* about Aunt Miriam?"

Mother was smiling, trying to hold back a laugh. "Well, what do you mean, exactly?"

Ruth looked severely at her sister. Lucy wasn't sure why. She also didn't quite know what to say.

After a pause, Lucy tried to put what she was feeling into words. "It's just that I. Well, I had a weird dream that Miriam was living in the walls. And she had friends with her, too. They were ALL living in there, all of these crazy, old ladies. And I tried to tell you about it in the middle of the night, but…."

Mother took Lucy's hand in her own. "Honey, I'm sorry you've had a bad dream. You know you can *always* come to me, day or night. But let's try to be charitable with Aunt Miriam. I know she's a little unusual, with all this *meat-eating* and the loud talking and carrying-on. But deep down, she's a nice lady and she's had a tough time."

Lucy angrily folded her arms. She gave a sigh. How could grown-ups be so dense, including her own mother? She didn't know what else to say, so she got up. "Okay, fine. I'm feeling better now. I'd better get dressed."

Mother gave Lucy another little hug. She promised the girls a good breakfast if they could make it down in the next 15 minutes or so. After that, she had a Goober consultation in the city and would be gone for the rest of the day.

"Don't worry," she said. "I will be back by dinner-time. And if you need anything, your Aunt Miriam is here."

As soon as Mother was gone, Lucy rushed over to Ruth. She grabbed her arm.

"Ouch! What's going on?"

"OK, you've GOT to help me!" said Lucy, a pleading look in her eyes.

"Help you with what?" asked Ruth.

"Just come here." Lucy pulled Ruth across their bedroom. She pointed to the wall, poking her finger at the wallpaper. "It was in here. This is where Miriam went in. There was like, a big hole with light coming out. Then Miriam and her helpers went *inside*."

Lucy was emphatically gesturing to the wall, near the dumbwaiter panel. She was ready to describe everything in detail, because she just knew that Ruth wouldn't understand.

Ruth surprised her by slowly approaching the wall. She lifted her arm to a particular spot. "Somehow, I know what you're talking about."

"You do?" asked Lucy.

"Yes, I think so. And this is the *soft spot*. It's where one finds the seam." Ruth ran her finger along a faint, green line. She moved her hand side-to-side, rubbing her finger slowly across the wall. Some of the green came off on her finger, and she smeared it back into the wall. "This green stuff is supposed to open up the seam. But it's not exactly fresh."

Lucy was speechless. How did her sister know these things? Were they both in the dream world now?

"Wait, that's not right." Ruth corrected the motion of her arm. Now she was moving her hand up and down, following the green line exactly. She could feel the wall reacting, vibrating under her touch. "Quick, help me!"

"But wait," said Lucy. "What are you doing? Are you sure you *want* to do that?" Now that it was happening, Lucy wasn't certain she wanted to find out. Nonetheless, she joined her sister. They both worked on the wall, softening it up and breaking it down.

They reached a frenzy of activity. Suddenly, Ruth said, "Here we go!" Then her arm disappeared into the wall, up to her shoulder. She looked back at her sister, eyes wide.

"Holy....!" Lucy covered her mouth before the whole phrase spilled out. "Wait, if you go in there, will you be able to come back?"

"I don't know, but you've got to come with me!" said Ruth. She hesitated for a moment. "At least we'll be together."

Chapter 17

Beyond the Wall

Downstairs, Mother was getting impatient. She had offered to make breakfast, but she didn't have time to dawdle. Not today.

"Ruth. Lucy, dear," she called out. "It's getting late!"

When she got no response, she took off her apron, laid it on the kitchen table, and headed upstairs.

Mother met Miriam on the stairs. She had never seen Miriam so cheery. "Good morning, Miriam. Have you seen the girls? They're supposed to be getting ready for school."

"Ah, yes. Of course," said Miriam. "Let me know if I can help, won't you?"

Mother paused for a moment. She gave a little smile. "Well, that would be wonderful if you could get the girls ready for school. I have an early appointment, and I've got to run."

"Fine, fine, my dear," said Miriam, smiling. "I can make sure they're ready and on time. No worries at all."

Mother grabbed her coat and purse. She called upstairs to say a quick goodbye to Lucy and Ruth. As she headed to the door, she smiled. "Thanks so much, Miriam!"

"Ow!" said Lucy. "You're stepping on my foot."

"Sorry." It was so dark Ruth and Lucy could barely make anything out. Still, Ruth knew they needed to go forward toward a very faint light. She took her sister's forearm and dragged her on. Ruth found it a little hard to breathe—the air seemed musty in here, like in a cave. She pushed on anyway.

It was getting harder to drag Lucy, who suddenly stopped in her tracks. "Wait, I just remembered. We're supposed to be eating breakfast. And we have to get to school."

"This is more important than school," said Ruth. She didn't sound like herself. Her voice was hollow and emotionless.

The light was not so faint anymore. The girls slowly made out the walls of a long hallway on either side of them.

Lucy pointed in horror at the walls. There were old-fashioned looking portraits hung at intervals. "I've seen those pictures before! That old woman and the girl? The old man? This is where I was in my dream…."

"Yes, I know. Or, I understand," said Ruth. She pulled her sister onward.

After a few more steps, they realized they were at the doorway of a room. Ruth poked her head in first, then Lucy peered in. "What is this place? It's certainly not the bathroom. It's not Mother and Father's room. What is it?"

Ruth gave a little sigh. She closed her hands around her sister's arms. "Don't you *get* any of this? This is NOT our regular house. This

96

is something else. Something Aunt Miriam has found. Or revealed." Ruth struggled to find the words. "If you read any actual books, you'd know that this kind of thing happens."

"Well!" answered Lucy. "No need to be snotty about it. I can see we've entered another, like, *dyemansion* or something."

Ruth started to correct her sister. "The word is dimen… oh, anyway. Come on."

They entered a small room. Built into each wall was a bookshelf, and in the center was an old-fashioned table. It looked like an ordinary room, like a small library. What was not so ordinary was the greenish light pouring out of the walls, the ceiling, even the round table. Everything gave off a faint glow.

Scattered across the table were objects the girls recognized: vials, jars, and dried plants they had seen among Miriam's stuff. Greenish vapor wafted from a large flask, giving off an earthy smell.

"This must be a potion of some kind," said Ruth. She sniffed the air. "I detect the aroma of motherwort leaves. And some other smells I can't identify."

"This is totally weird," said Lucy. "Like a mad scientist's lab."

Ruth was pointing to a book, opened up wide in the middle of the table. Of course, it was The Big Black Book.

"Look at this," said Ruth, trying to keep calm. She pointed to a blue line drawing in the book. Lucy hung back. She wasn't sure she wanted to get any closer.

"Now things are becoming clearer," whispered Ruth. There was

a drawing of their house, labeled 566 Chenery Street, Glen Park. Underneath, another address was crossed out.

Lucy started to speak before she even knew what to say. "You don't think. I mean, is it possible that Aunt Miriam is kind of... like, doing something bad with our house? Like, something evil or sinister? I mean, I don't believe in wizards and stuff like that. But is Miriam a....?"

Ruth was quiet.

Out of the corner of her eye, Lucy saw something dark and hairy moving through the room. "Aaah!" She screamed.

They heard a resonant voice behind them. It was Miriam. "I believe the word you're looking for is... WITCH."

Chapter 18

Darkhouse

Miriam let out a laugh. She seemed taller and grander than ever, her curly hair backlit by the green glowing light. "My, my. We've caught some mice at play. Oh, and I see they've been poking their little noses where they don't belong?" Miriam picked up her Black Book, closing it abruptly.

Lucy and Ruth were frozen in place. They should have known Miriam wouldn't be far behind them, thought Ruth. The old lady knew everything. Oh, and it seemed she was a witch.

Several glowing eyes appeared out of the darkness. Then there were more eyes. They got closer and closer.

Lucy gave a little whimper, clutching at her sister's arm. This was all too much for her. The girls started to edge backwards.

When they reached the hallway, they broke into a sprint. "We've got to find Mom!" yelled Lucy.

"First. We've got to. Get out. Of here," said Ruth, trying to catch her breath. The air was danker than ever. It was a musky animal smell that made it hard to breathe. She pushed ahead and found the place in the wall they had come through. "Where is that opening?"

"It must be here somewhere," said Lucy, running her hands over the wall. She couldn't find the seam anywhere.

"Wait a minute," said Miriam, cautiously approaching the girls. In her arms, she had her loving cats. In a quiet voice, she said, "I'm very sorry, my dears. I didn't mean to startle you...."

Lucy refused to hear another word. She dove headlong into the wall, guessing at where the opening was. Instead of going through the wall, she bumped her head and crumpled to the ground.

"Lucy, are you all right?" Ruth shouted, but she couldn't move a muscle. It seemed that ropes or something had sprung up around her. They wrapped around her arms, pinning her down. She looked over at her sister. She was covered, too—in dark, leafy, crawling vines.

"NOW, my dearest nieces," said Miriam. She stepped forward, lighting up the hallway with her presence. "Sorry I have to do this, but I need your attention. If you promise to stay still and *listen*, just for a minute, I will let you go. No harm done."

Ruth knew her aunt better than anyone in the family—at least, she thought she did. She didn't think she'd actually harm them, even if she was a witch. Finally, she spoke up. "Okay, okay. But please, you have to explain what's going on. ALL of it."

Looking sternly at the girls, Miriam waved her hand in the air. The creepy vines crept back down. "Fine, fine. Please follow me."

Miriam strolled back toward the mysterious room, lighting the way as she went. Ruth and Lucy hesitantly followed.

"My, my. The princesses are awake," said an unfamiliar voice.

Miriam waved her hand, and the room lit up. Two women stepped out of the shadows.

"I know you," said Lucy quietly. "You're from my dream."

"Yes. These are two of my oldest friends, Ms. Biddy Entwistle and Ms. Sally Snipwick. They are here for a few days, helping on a special project," explained Miriam. The ladies each gave a little bow. Ms. Entwistle had a friendly smile on her plump face. Ms. Snipwick seemed more serious.

"Witches *always* travel in threes, especially where there's something important afoot," said Ruth. She placed her hands on the round table, steadying herself. "So I'd like to know: what in the *world* is going on here?"

Miriam spoke in a soothing voice. "Well, the ladies and I are actually not big fans of the term *Witches*. We think of ourselves more as historians, uncovering things from the past. Like anything magical, or even out of the ordinary, you have to SEE it to believe it."

"Wait, are you going to show them *everything*?" said Ms. Snipwick, angrily. "What if they tell their parents?" Then she added in a whisper, "Or report us to the police?"

Miriam gave her friend a reproachful look. "It's time, Sally. It's time. If you don't want to be a part of it, that's your choice."

Ms. Snipwick stepped back into the shadows, leaving the others.

"I'm with you," said Ms. Entwistle. She and Miriam joined hands. Bowing their heads, they made a low chanting sound. It sounded like

bees buzzing deep underground. *Buuuurrrrrzzzzuuuuummmmm.*

Nothing happened. Lucy and Ruth looked around, noting the many books on the shelves. Lucy cleared her throat. Ruth folded her arms. Her legs ached, and she wished she had a chair. Then she had a thought, and quietly joined hands with the ladies.

Slowly the light in the room changed. Before the girls even knew what was happening, the walls of the room had disappeared. Ruth looked up, and the ceiling was gone, too. Somehow they were all still standing in a group: Ruth, Miriam and Ms. Entwistle all holding hands. And Lucy had joined hands, too.

As the light changed again, they were standing outside in a field. Overhead, the sun was shining and the sky was a pale blue. They could hear birds singing and insects chirping. The air was fresh; the musty smell had gone.

"It's beautiful," said Ruth.

"This is like a movie," whispered Lucy. "It seems SO real but also, not real at all."

Ruth nodded.

The ladies kept chanting. The sun went down and rose again. Then the same thing happened faster.

Now they were standing in the living room of a house. It *almost* looked like their own house, but it was super old-timey. The living room was filled with cushiony, old-fashioned furniture. The lamps were flickering.

"This totally looks like our house," said Lucy. Then she clapped a hand over her mouth. She was worried speaking aloud would break the spell, or whatever this was.

Miriam half-opened her eyes, looking over at the girls. She gave them a reassuring nod. *Everything is okay.*

All sorts of things were happening around them, in this house. The walls were changing color and shape. There were fleeting views of people going up and down the stairs. Lucy noticed the beautiful clothes worn by a tall, haughty lady. She wore a necklace of shiny pearls.

"I know that lady!" blurted out Lucy. "I saw her in a painting, in my dream."

The scene continued to play out. The beautiful lady was sitting

alone in a darkened room. Her eyes shone even more brightly than her pearl necklace. Then an older man was shouting at the lady. He had something dark and sinister in his hand as he came down the curved stairway. There was a flash of anger. After the lady was gone, Lucy felt a tear rolling down her cheek. There were mourners dressed in black, passing through the house. It was a wake, part of a funeral.

Everything was moving so fast. The scenes were happy, then sad. The emotions Lucy and Ruth felt were almost too much to handle.

Things slowly became a little more familiar. "Oh my God!" cried Lucy, unable to stay quiet. "This IS our house. And that's Father!" It was their young Father from pictures, before he had a beard. He looked skinny and jumpy.

"I want to see Mom!" said Ruth. Soon enough, there was Mother. She looked almost the same, though her face was shinier.

"Look at Mom's HUGE glasses," said Lucy, laughing. "And those totally cheesy earrings."

Both girls were silent. They saw a baby crawling across the wooden floorboards. She looked *so cute*, thought Lucy. The plump baby had blue eyes and little wisps of blonde hair. She wore a cloth diaper, with a pink flower safety pin.

"Holy…" said Ruth. "That's you, Lucy."

"Yeah, it's ME."

Soon they saw little Lucy again, trying to climb the stairs. She must be almost one year old. She was dressed all in pink. Then she turned and crawled toward Mother, who was sitting in a rocking chair, waiting to greet her.

Ruth got a strange feeling. A feeling that made her suddenly queasy, down in the pit of her stomach. She grabbed her side, blurting out a few words. "Where am I? That's YOU, Lucy, but I should be there too!"

Now the image of Mother was yelling. They weren't sure whom she was yelling at, but she looked really upset. It was hard for Ruth and Lucy to watch.

Everything went dark again, in an instant. Lucy grabbed her sister's hand tight.

Miriam suddenly stopped chanting, dropping her friends' hands. She had a worried look on her face.

Still, they heard their Mother shouting from somewhere. "Luuuucy! Ruuuuthie! Miriam? Where ARE you? I can see your backpacks and coats. Are you HERE?"

With that, the spell was broken. It was really Mother calling from downstairs, in real life. Right now.

Miriam looked truly shocked, something the girls had never seen. She gripped Ms. Entwistle's arm. "Well, goodnight! Hattie's back home, and she's sure to find us out. We haven't a moment to lose."

Chapter 19

Glen Park Elementary

Miriam reopened the seam in the wall with a deft movement of her hand. She took Lucy's arm, and helped her through the opening. She did the same for Ruth. Before she let go of her niece's hand, she said, "Okay, girls. Now, please remember what we talked about. And I promise: Nothing bad will happen."

Ruth nodded. "Ok, we understand."

Lucy hesitated. "Well, okay. Yes, I understand. But you *have* to tell Mother everything."

Miriam gave them a pleading look, her lips pursed. She reached out a hand and waved. It almost seemed like she was saying goodbye. Then she closed up the seam from her side of the wall.

The girls were dazed after everything they had seen. Lucy stumbled over to her bed and sat down. Ruth followed, sitting next to her sister. It was nice but strange to be back in their own room.

"Wow, you never sit on my bed," said Lucy.

"Um, yeah. Things feel a little different today, don't they?"

Lucy didn't know what to say. So they just sat there, holding hands.

Their bedroom door opened, and Mother stepped in. "What in the blessed name of…. what are you both still doing here, in your pajamas?" She stepped forward, waving her hands in the air. "And where is your Aunt Miriam?"

Ruth and Lucy had rehearsed what they were going to say. Ruth stood up to deliver the first line. "Mother, we are very sorry. One of Aunt Miriam's closest friends has taken ill, so Miriam had to leave in a hurry."

Then Lucy chimed in. "That's right, Mom. Miriam had an *oblation* to go…."

Mother looked quizzically at her daughter. This didn't sound like Lucy at all. "Um. I think you mean, *obligation*?"

Lucy's eyes opened wide. "YES. I mean an obligation. For that reason, she was unable to bring us to school." She seemed lost in thought for a moment. Then she added, "So that's why we're late."

They were *very* late, Mother pointed out. It was lucky that her appointment in the city had been cancelled, she said, or she didn't know what would've happened.

Mother made sure they got ready in a hurry, standing guard as the girls got dressed.

In less than 20 minutes they were off to school.

It felt like a super long day at Glen Park Elementary, even though the girls had missed most of it.

In Mr. Tembruell's class, Ruth's mind wandered. She needed time to process the things she had seen. Or was it that Miriam and her friends had *shown* them these things, like a super realistic video you could almost reach out and touch. In any case, it was like watching the history of their house. Before the house was built, and the people that had lived there before. The images were beautiful and happy, then sad, and then totally weird. And then there was the kicker: Where was *she* in all of this? Where was Baby Ruth?

"Ruth? Ruth?" It was Mr. Tembruell's voice, coming from somewhere far away. "Earth to Ruth Hoogablased: Can we get your attention, please?"

Ruth looked up. Oh, no! The whole class was staring at her. One of Lucy's friends, a silly girl named Amelia, was pointing and giggling.

"Sorry, Mr. T," said Ruth. "It's been a long day." She wondered how her sister was faring across the hall in Ms. Schaeffer's class.

"Okay, no worries. Just want to make sure everything's all right?" said Mr. T. He gave her a quick smile. "Now, let's get back to our

Joogle Docs, everyone."

Ruth zoned out again. She was still thinking about this morning.

Then she got an idea, typing in a search on her school laptop.

are witches **real** ?

are witches **immortal**
are witches **good**
are witches **supernatural**
are witches **beautiful**
are witches **bad**
are **all** witches **bad**
what are witches **balls**
where are witches **buried in salem**
what are witches **beliefs**

Joogle Search   I'm Feeling Lucky

Chapter 20

A House
Disturbed

That evening, Mother laid out every vegetable she could find: bright green zucchini, a dark eggplant, mixed greens, shallots, vine-ripened tomatoes, and organic purple garlic. She had decided to take back the cooking duties for the time being. Though she couldn't put her finger on it, she felt that Miriam's meat-heavy meals weren't good for the family's health.

As Mother washed, peeled, chopped, spiced, and cooked, a rich veggie aroma filled the kitchen. "Ah, that's more like it," she said to herself. "Tonight we get back to basics with some *ratatouille.*"

The smell brought the cats into the kitchen. They seemed restless and out of sorts. Frankie marched up and down the kitchen, irritably rubbing her back against everything she could find.

"What's going on with these cats?" asked Mother as Lucy entered the kitchen. Lucy sat down at the table. She looked tired. "I don't know. Maybe it's because Miriam is gone? But she *should* be back by now."

"I see," said Mother. Her intuition told her that *something* odd was going on. "Is everything all right? I expected to hear from Miriam by now."

Lucy wondered if she should tell Mother everything. After all, Mom was a considerate person. Maybe she'd understand. She was always saying it was important to be accepting of other kinds of people. Did that apply to *witches*, too? Lucy felt a pang of guilt for not telling, but she wasn't sure she could explain anyway.

As she was pondering, Ruth appeared at the doorway. She looked nervous. She motioned to Lucy, begging her to come into the living room.

"Why?" whispered Lucy. "What's wrong now?"

"Come on, we've got trouble," said Ruth.

Lucy and Ruth excused themselves, saying they had some homework to check before dinner. Then Ruth grabbed her sister's arm, dragging her upstairs.

When they reached the upstairs landing, a terrible odor greeted them. It smelled totally putrid and rotten. "Oh my God!" said Lucy. "Is that coming from…?"

Ruth nodded, pulling her sister into their bedroom.

They had never seen Aunt Miriam so panicked. In her hands was a large broom, which she was waving furiously at the bedroom wall. But it wasn't really their bedroom wall anymore. It was a giant, frothing, bubbling mess of greenish brown goop spilling out of a gaping hole in the wall, where the *seam* had been. It looked like a big, disgusting mouth.

"I can't keep this stuff back much longer!" shouted Miriam. She was trying desperately to stop the slime, but the slime was winning.

Ruth and Lucy were speechless.

"I'm searching as fast as I can!" Another voice shouted from the other side of the room. It was Ms. Entwistle, wrapped up in her scarves. She was paging furiously through the Big Black Book. Then she picked up another book. "I don't see anything in here about stopping this... whatever this is! If only Ms. Snipwick were here—I bet *she'd* know what to do."

The girls gasped as the slime spilled onto the floor. A sickening smell hit them, like the house had spit up a thousand rotten eggs.

"We must have gone too far," admitted Miriam. She still had her broom, but it was covered with loamy brown goo. "Now, we've got to reseal this wall and turn the enchantment backwards, somehow. But there's only the two of us..."

Little Ruth quietly stepped forward. She raised her arm, pointing at the bubbling mess. "I know what to do."

For a moment, Miriam and Ms. Entwistle were silent. Then Miriam shouted. "Really? Then for the love of Hecate, get in there and do it!"

———————————————————————

The bubbling, churning sliminess was creeping up the carpeting.

Ruth was unfazed. She seemed like a different person—not a little nine-year-old, but someone much older and wiser. She spoke resolutely. "Okay, as you can see the House is unhappy. We've uncovered too much, and now it's spewing out everything in its guts." With a determined look, she added, "What we have to do is reverse that."

Obediently, Miriam and Ms. Entwistle stood at Ruth's side. Without any prompting, all three joined hands. With a nod from Ruth, they concentrated their thoughts. Ruth narrated what they were doing. "All of the things we've seen about this house… all the stored memories, happy and sad. The people who lived here before, and the things we have seen. We've got to put them back."

The slime continued to flow, though it had slowed.

Lucy was still in shock. She hadn't moved a muscle since entering the room. As the gooey stuff reached her shoes, she jumped back. She wanted to cry out for Mother downstairs, but couldn't find her voice.

Ruth pressed on. She thought back to the old-fashioned house with the kind lady in her chair, waiting for her child. It was a happy memory, and now she was putting it back in its place. She was surprised to feel a little hand in hers. Was it the hand of the young child?

No, it was Lucy. She joined hands with her sister. "I want to help," said Lucy. All four of them kept up their concentration, channeling their thoughts. They were traveling back through the memories of the House.

A dark thought crept back into Ruth's mind. Again, she could see Mother. She must be about 25 years old, wearing a sunny flower dress. And those big glasses. She was typing at a big, boxy looking computer in their living room. She looked up, and a little girl with blonde hair who must be Lucy ran toward her. Oh, the expression on each of their faces! They were so happy in each other's company. Then a young version of Father joined them and they were singing songs and laughing. But there was no little Ruth to be seen anywhere. How could that be?

Ruth opened her eyes. She couldn't take any more of this—it was too painful. She dropped hands with Lucy. Ruth slumped over, practically falling to the ground.

"What's wrong with her?" yelled Lucy. She took her sister's arm and half-led, half-carried her over to the bed. Ruth's face was white as a sheet. All of the energy seemed to have drained from her legs and arms. Ruth fell onto the mattress.

Suddenly, there was a sucking sound coming from the hole in the wall. Then a rumble shook the floors and walls. A cloud of rancid gas spread out through the room. Apparently, the House was passing a huge belch. The slime stopped, almost like it had been turned off with a button.

Miriam and Ms. Entwistle looked relieved. They turned their attention to Ruth, who was lying prostrate on the bed. "Ruth, dear," said Miriam. "You must stay awake now. Stay with us, my dearest child...."

Ruth's eyes fluttered and then she passed out cold.

"You've got to do something!" cried Lucy, waving her arms at Miriam. "Aren't you a Witch? So cast a spell or give her a healing potion, or something?" Lucy's voice was frantic.

Miriam's face was a mix of concern and embarrassment. Apparently, she didn't know *what* to do. She started to mutter to herself. "Well, I could... No, that wouldn't work. Well, what about tincture of motherwort?"

Lucy spoke up in a determined voice. "Okay, enough. You don't know *what* you're doing and I'm going to get Mother. We're going to tell her everything."

Chapter 21

The Council of Witches

At the first sign of trouble, Ms. Snipwick had disappeared from the Hoogablased house. Being the sensible one of the group was a burden, Sally Snipwick told herself, but *someone* had to do it. In a flash, she was down on Chenery Street heading as quickly as she could toward the nearby neighborhood of Noe Valley. She had to see Ms. Tituba, the leader of The Council of Witches. As luck would have it, there was a Council meeting this evening.

As she reached her destination, The Noe Valley Center for Mindful Meditation was just opening its back doors onto Castro Street. A small sign written in special ink that only Council Members could see spelled it out.

May Day Meeting of
The Council of Witches

Ladies young and old, along with several skittish men, were streaming in the back door. Most of them carried yoga mats under their arms. They greeted each other with a hearty "Merry meet," which was the typical salutation. Ms. Snipwick grabbed a candle and removed her shoes, blending in with the other witches. Then the group of thirty or more, along with quite a few cats, gathered in a large, darkened room at the back of the Center.

With lit candles at their sides, each witch unrolled his or her yoga mat and sat cross-legged. There was a period of laughter and chatter until the Council of Witches was finally called to order.

Ms. Tituba was the eldest Member and leader of the Council. She quickly got the attention of the audience, and sang out in a beautiful voice. "Hear ye, hear ye. Calling all sorceresses, enchantresses, necromancers, and conjurers."

The whole audience responded. "WE HEAR YOU."

Ms. Tituba continued. "Calling all bewitchers, hags, crones, and soothsayers."

Again the audience shouted. "WE HEAR YOU."

Ms. Tituba raised her voice. "Calling all beldams, charmers, sea witches, shamans and shrews."

"WE HEAR YOU."

Ms. Tituba was practically crying out. "Calling all the WITCHES of San Francisco!"

"WE HEAR YOU. TELL US WHAT YOU SEE!"

"I see trouble... toil and trouble," responded Ms. Tituba. Then she

got right down to business. "Fellow witches: We have an urgent matter before the Council. Please direct your attention to the screen."

There was murmuring from the audience as an old-fashioned screen was pulled down. Instead of a video presentation, the screen lit up from within. It showed the image of an old, Victorian style house: The Hoogablased home. The image changed to reveal the interior of the house. The picture was constantly shifting, showing the comings and goings of many, varied families.

There were *Oohs* and *Aahs* from the audience. Few of the assembled witches had ever seen what they were watching now.

Ms. Tituba cleared her throat. "For those of you who have heard whisperings and murmurings... yes, it is true. A group of our San Francisco witches has uncovered an actual haunted house, a DARKHOUSE."

The *Oohs* and *Aahs* from the group turned into *Wows* and *Reallys?*

Ms. Tituba continued. "The principal Witch is a Ms. Miriam Levings, who most recently lived downtown."

The Council Secretary made a whimpering little noise. Then she spoke up. "Ah, sorry. Her name is Miriam Levin. Not Levings."

Ms. Tituba shot the secretary a glance. "Fine. It's Ms. Miriam *Levin*, along with her friends, Ms. Entwistle and Ms. Snipwick, who is here tonight."

There was applause from the room.

Ms. Snipwick emerged from the audience. Carrying her candle, she walked to the front of the room. She spoke to the group in a loud voice, trying to reach every witch in the audience. "My fellow witches, I bring good news! My friend, Miriam Levin, who was until recently a research librarian at the public library, has uncovered an error in the literature. She found a mistake in *Bierce's Compendium of Mysterious Events & Places.*"

Ms. Snipwick held up her candle. "In fact, Miriam's family home is a prominent Glen Park house with a troubled past. Forty years ago, there was a murder. A beautiful, young Witch was killed by her jealous husband."

There was shouting and cursing from the group. They hated to hear about the murder of a fellow witch. The persecution of witches was all too common, and most of the ladies had experienced it in some form.

Ms. Snipwick continued. "It was the unfortunate witch's daughter who later placed a curse on the house. And that is what my friends and I have uncovered. A real, honest to goodness Darkhouse, right here in San Francisco."

There was whispering and chatter from the audience.

Then a small, mousey looking woman in the audience stood up. She addressed her remarks to Ms. Snipwick. "Um, excuse me. But I must ask... How do you know all of this, about the House's history, and so on?" The mousey looking woman sat down.

Ms. Snipwick thought for a moment. It was now, or never. She would have to reveal everything. "Well, that's the thing. You see, we three witches—Ms. Levin, Ms. Entwistle and I—have already begun the Enchantment of the House. We are trying to reveal the curse...."

There were gasps from the audience now.

The mousey woman quickly stood up again. "Do you mean to tell us that you have gone ahead and opened up an enchanted house? Without the guidance or permission of the Council?" The woman seemed truly upset.

"Yes," said Ms. Snipwick, admitting her guilt. "I'm afraid we've already revealed the history of the house. But you should see what that history looks like—the lush gardens and the beautiful libraries, and other rooms we have just started to...."

There was more shouting from the audience. Apparently, they did not like this one bit. "I know Miriam Levin," exclaimed one older lady. "She's NOT much of a witch, I can tell you. She's a half-baked old hag, and she was *fired* from the public library."

A tall, elegant woman stood up. "Never mind that," she said. "Do you realize the DANGER that has been exposed here? What if something goes wrong with this house?"

The jeering and shouting continued.

Ms. Tituba finally had to bang her large shoe against the lectern at the front of the room. "Quiet, quiet, QUIET! Now, honorable Members... Please. This is why we have called you together today, to ask your approval—even if it comes very late—and to support our fellow witches in any way we can. I have spoken with Ms. Snipwick, who has assured me that, in time, this House will be of great value to the Council."

Ms. Tituba and some of her allies were finally able to calm the group down. Then the leader called for a formal Vote, as the Council did in matters of great importance. Ms. Tituba read the proposition aloud:

WE THE COUNCIL OF WITCHES SUPPORT THE ENCHANTMENT OF THE HOUSE AT 566 CHENERY STREET, PLEDGING OUR GUIDANCE AND SUPPORT TO Ms. Levin, Ms. Snipwick, and Ms. Entwistle, PROVIDED THAT PRECAUTIONS ARE STRICTLY FOLLOWED. AYE OR NAYE?

With that the Council passed out ballots and began voting.

As she got ready to depart, Ms. Snipwick whispered to her old confidant, Ms. Tituba. "I hope you can pull this off. Miriam's in over her head, we all are. I can just feel it."

"We'll see, my dear. We shall see."

Ms. Snipwick's candle had burned down to a nub. She blew it out and took her leave, saying she would await the results of the Council's vote.

Chapter 22

Mother

Ruth was still lying on her sister's bed, passed out cold. Her breathing was slow and labored. At least she was breathing, thought Lucy.

"But how did this happen?" asked Mother, reaching for her telephone. She said she would call 911 if Ruth didn't come to.

Lucy had never seen Mother's face so serious with concern. "It's a long story," said Lucy, looking over at Miriam. Her friend, Ms. Entwistle, had disappeared in a hurry.

Miriam's face had turned from profound embarrassment to intense concentration. She stepped forward with a small flask in her hand. "This is a homemade mixture of herbs. It'll work like smelling salts, but even stronger."

"No! No more of that witchy stuff," shouted Lucy. "This is how we got into this mess to begin with!"

Mother turned her gaze on Miriam. It was a look that said: *You had better explain, and fast.*

"Hattie, my dear," said Miriam, sitting down on the bed next to poor Ruth. "As your daughter said, it's a long story." Without further warning, Miriam opened the vial and a pungent smell wafted through the room.

Ruth sat up like a shot. "What's that smell?" she said, looking around. "Is it... tincture of motherwort?" Ruth slowly became aware of her surroundings. Her Mother, Aunt Miriam, and Lucy were all looking at her.

"Oh, thank God you're all right," said Mother. She wiped her daughter's warm brow with a cloth.

"Man, I'm so glad you're back. Now we've got to tell Mom everything," said Lucy, gripping her sister's hand. "About the seam, and the weird visions and the slime and... well, everything."

Miriam knew it was time for her to explain, as best she could. In a quiet, confessional voice she described the project she had started. She had found a floor plan of the Hoogablased home and was researching its history, trying to discover its mysterious past. Her intentions were good, she promised.

Miriam's story sounded partly believable and partly crazy, thought Lucy. Miriam hadn't mentioned that she was a Witch, of course. She made it sound like she was a history professor or something.

Everyone was surprised when Ruth spoke up. "I've kind of known all along. About the house, and the garden, and everything. I just got this feeling. You see, Auntie Miriam isn't a bad person or anything. She's just led an unusual life. And I think we should be supportive of different lifestyles, don't you?"

Mother was silently taking all of this in. Her daughters couldn't tell if she was totally confused or completely furious. It was impossible to tell.

Just then, the doorbell rang downstairs. It rang again, and there was an insistent pounding on the door.

Mother sighed, and got up. She took Lucy and Ruth by the hand. "Okay, I'm going to get the door. Now, Miriam," she addressed the older lady. "Could you please stay right here? I know you can disappear in an instant, but please stay put this time. Okay?"

Miriam nodded. "I'll be right here, my dear."

"I can see your car out front, so I knew you all were home." It was the UPS man, Big Mike, at the front door. "Everything okay?"

Mother and her daughters looked like they had been through the ringer. The girls had bags under their eyes, and Mother seemed like she might jump out of her own skin.

"I'm sorry, Mike," said Mother. "It's been a long day. Please come in for a minute."

Big Mike had a happy, infectious charm. Everyone in the neighborhood said so. Soon, he got a smile out of Ruth and Lucy. Then he produced a large, flat envelope from under his arm. "This is an Extra Special Delivery," he explained. "To be delivered Same Day. Do you know how much that costs?"

The package was addressed to Ms. Miriam Levin, 566 Chenery Street.

Mother thanked Mike and took the package, saying, "Yes, I'll take care of this."

"Absolutely, Mrs. H." replied Mike, winking. "And a good evening to you all."

———————————————————

"Aren't you going to give Miriam her package?" asked Ruth. She knew Mother was upset with their aunt, but she wasn't sure how far it would go.

Mother looked surprised. "Yes, of course I will." After a pause she said, "Of course, I need to speak with her first. I guess you two had better come, too."

Mother hurried up the stairs, with Lucy and Ruth in tow.

"Do you think she's going to kick Miriam out?" whispered Lucy to her sister.

"I don't know. I really don't know."

Chapter 23

The Attic

Miriam had packed all of her books, plants, violin, and other belongings back into two medium-sized bags. The bedroom looked practically empty. The cats were milling around the room, hissing and whining. They clearly didn't want to leave their new home.

"Well, it's the story of my life," said Miriam, not looking at anyone in particular. "Every time I find something good, it slips away. Of course, it's my own fault. Now I'll be homeless again, but I'm used to it...." She looked around the room to see if her words were having any effect. Then she glanced over at Ruth, and at little Lucy. A tear formed in the corner of Miriam's eye and rolled down her cheek. She realized that she would miss her nieces terribly.

Mother explained that she was very sorry, but it was best if Miriam found another place to live. "Of course, we will help you if we can. Why don't we go down to the kitchen and pack a bag of supplies to take with you, for starters?"

"Fine, fine," said Miriam. She hoisted her bags over her shoulder and headed downstairs.

The whole group gathered in the kitchen. Lucy and Ruth sat with Miriam, as Mother searched the cupboards.

Miriam surprised everyone by quietly reaching around to the back of her head. With a ripping sound, she quickly lifted up her black, curly hair. It

was a wig. Without it, she was completely bald. She looked even more striking than ever.

"Oh, like, WOW!" exclaimed Lucy. "You look really…." She didn't complete her thought.

"I think you look beautiful," said Ruth. She came around the table, standing beside Miriam to show her support. "And we all know you were sick before."

"Soon, my hair will grow back—if I keep up with my herbal remedies. Of course, I need the plants from my garden. I mean, *your* garden." Miriam looked longingly out the kitchen window. The garden was in full bloom.

Mother's face was twitching. Then she made a decision. "Okay, okay. I've changed my mind. We are *family* and family sticks together, no matter what. Miriam, you may stay here if you'd like, as long as you follow some sensible…"

"Yay!" Ruth was overjoyed, giving Miriam a hug. Lucy was surprised to find that she felt happy and relieved, too.

Of course, no one was more relieved than Miriam, who let out a big sigh.

"Hey, in all the commotion, we forgot to eat dinner," said Mother, standing up. She was smiling. "I'll start heating up the ratatouille."

Surprisingly, Miriam joined her. "That sounds... um, delicious."

Everyone took big portions of ratatouille, including Miriam. She couldn't help but make a little joke as the dish was passed around. "Ratatouille. Does it have RAT in it?"

Ruth giggled. "No, of course not."

"Does it have... squirrel? Or gopher, or any other type of tasty rodent?"

"No, it's all vegetables. It's a vegetarian dish."

Miriam took another bite. "And it's delicious, all the same."

All of a sudden, Mother stood up at the table. "Oh, my! I forgot the package. The package for Miriam." She quickly fetched the big, flat envelope. She delivered it into Miriam's hands.

Miriam had a penknife in her hand. She deftly cut open the envelope, and took out a sheaf of yellowed papers. Then she quietly read over the first page. Her expression turned from concern to joy as she pored over it. She was practically singing out when she read the letter aloud to the family:

Dear Ms. Miriam Levin and friends,

One behalf of the San Francisco Council of Historians, I wish to congratulate you on your research. It appears that you have uncovered the mysterious history of one of our city's most prominent but least known houses, 566 Chenery Street, Glen Park.

Furthermore, we salute its owners, The Hoogablased family, on their attentive care of the home.

Please find enclosed a check from the Council to complete the research on the structure and its history. We request a full report following our guidelines and safe practices (see enclosed information) to be delivered at Noe Valley Center for Mindful Meditation in six months' time.

With further congratulations, we look forward to great things.

Sincerely,
Ms. Tituba
President,
The Council

At the bottom of the letter, Miriam saw a note written in invisible ink, which only she could see.

P.S. Don't screw this up. The Witches are counting on you! —T.

"Finally, some recognition for my…" said Miriam to herself. She was so excited she could hardly contain herself. As they finished dinner, Miriam told the family her plans. First, she would use the Council's money to pay off that despicable landlord, Mr. Pappas, and the other Angry Bill Collectors. She couldn't have them hounding her all her life. Any money left over she would use for her *research*, as she put it.

"Maybe you could start a school for… historical research," said Ruth. She winked at her aunt.

"No, don't do that," said Lucy, shaking her head. "You could do anything, even buy your own house with that money!"

Miriam smiled. "No, my dears. I'd very much like to stay right here with you." (Of course, it was not nearly enough money to buy a house in this super expensive town, but the girls didn't need to know that.)

As they were clearing their plates and prepping the dishes, they heard a voice from the living room. "Helloooo. Anybody here?"

It was Father. But he wasn't expected for several days! Lucy and Ruth got up excitedly. "I can't wait to tell him all the things that have happened!"

Before they could rush in, Mother gave them a little advice. "Well, girls. Why don't you let *me* explain this whole little story. Okay?"

Ruth and Lucy nodded. That really was for the best.

Father looked exhausted as he sat down to a late dinner. There was a brief moment of shock at seeing Miriam without her wig, but he took it in stride. Then Father explained why he was back home so early. Business was shaky for Goober, and an important deal in Sacramento had fallen through.

"Money might be tight for a while. But we'll manage, somehow," said Father. "Now, I've talked enough. Tell me what's been going on around here. Anything exciting?"

"Oh, nothing much!" said Mother, a little too quickly.

"Yeah. Same old, same old." Ruth and Lucy were smiling at each other. "All good!"

"Glad to hear *someone's* had a good week," said Father. He took another helping of ratatouille. "This is truly tasty."

After Father had gulped down his food, Miriam fetched her violin. She gave a rousing rendition of *Friend of the Devil*, with Father joining in.

"I know that's one of your favorites," said Miriam. She looked around at the family. "By the way, I have something to ask you all. Or maybe, better yet, to show you?"

"What now?" thought Mother. But she held her tongue, and agreed to see whatever Miriam had to show them.

Miriam took the family upstairs. In the middle of the hallway, she reached up and opened a panel in the ceiling. A rickety staircase folded down. A large, plump figure was coming down the staircase, which spooked everyone.

"Who on Earth is that?" asked Father.

Miriam introduced the giggly woman to the family. "This is my dearest friend, Ms. Biddy Entwistle. We go way back."

"Very pleased to meet you all," said Ms. Entwistle, winking at Lucy and Ruth.

"Are we going up into the attic?" asked Ruth.

"Yes, now this is the really big surprise," said Miriam. She led the

whole family up the stairs into the attic. "We've been working on it for some time, and I think it's ready for your viewing pleasure. You see, Biddy and I would like to live up here, if that's all right with you. And we would be happy to kick in some rent, too!"

Without further ado, Miriam showed them the room. The attic was completely transformed. The boxes were gone, and in their place was beautiful old furniture. All of Miriam's books & curious objects were arranged on shelves and tables. The room was very cozy and very *witchy*, thought Ruth and Lucy.

"Whoa, it's so YOU," said Ruth, admiring the books. "And I totally want to hang out up here."

"I guess it's nice," said Lucy. "But it needs a little *color*. There's not one thing in here that's not black or gray. What about some pink, for a change!"

Miriam nodded. "Well, if it needs some color, you'll have to visit." She tried out her sitting chair in its new location. "I feel like I'm home, sweet home at last."

The family lingered a while in the attic room. There were plenty of books and strange objects to look over, including a full-size black cauldron. (*What's that for?* said Mother to herself.)

Soon it was time for bed, and everyone said their "goodnights." As she was leaving, Mother pulled Miriam aside. "You know we're glad to have you," said Mother. "But I think if you're going to stay here *permanently*, it's time to tell Ruth everything."

Miriam looked serious for a moment. "Yes, of course. I'll do it tonight."

Chapter 24

That's The Truth, Ruth

Lucy and Ruth got their beds ready, with a little help from their parents. It was good to have their own room back, said Lucy. Ruth agreed that it was probably better this way.

Mother tucked in Lucy with a big hug. Then she visited Ruth in her old army cot. "It's been quite a day," said Mother, stroking Ruth's dark hair. "Sleep tight."

With that, the girls dozed off.

In the middle of the night, Ruth awoke with a start. She had a funny feeling that something or someone was waiting for her, out in the hallway. She found her black slippers and quietly tiptoed to the door, making sure not to disturb Lucy.

She found Mother and Miriam standing quietly in the middle of the hall. Mother had a strange expression on her face. "We were just discussing whether we should wake you, my dear."

"I know what you want to tell me," said Ruth, without hesitation.

"Do you, really?" A smile played across Miriam's lips. "Well, I thought you might."

Mother gave Ruth a tight embrace, saying, "Miriam has something to tell you. It's something I've known about for a long time, and we think you're ready to hear it." She smiled, and hugged Ruthie closer. "Just remember, I'll always be here for you. We all will."

"I know," said Ruth. "I love you."

Mother left the two of them alone. Then it was Miriam's turn to give Ruth a long, tender hug. "Oh, it's been so long and so difficult. But it's finally time to tell you the truth, Ruth. I'm so sorry for not being there when you were little; it's something I just couldn't handle. I hope it's all worked out for the best. Just know that I am here now. And I will be forevermore."

Ruth wasn't ready to call her Mother, even though Miriam was indeed her true, natural birth mother. She had sensed it for a little while. All the signs had certainly pointed to it.

Ruth took Miriam's hand. She had so many things to say that she barely knew where to begin. "Could we go upstairs? I have so many questions."

"Yes, of course. I have some things waiting to show you."

As they ascended the little staircase once again, Ruth burst out with her first question. She just couldn't wait. "I know you're my mother. So, my father is...."

"Jack. My ex-husband, Jack. Ours was an unhappy marriage, I'm sorry to say."

"And that means Lucy's not really my sister. She's my cousin," added Ruth.

"Yes. Since you are almost the same age, that seemed the only way to… handle things."

Ruth was trying to absorb all of this. She summoned the last of her courage and posed the question she really wanted to ask. "So, if you're a witch. Well, I know you don't care for that word. But if you're a witch, then am I one too?"

Miriam smiled. "Well, that depends. I'd say there's a strong possibility. It does run on the maternal bloodline, you see."

"Awwwesome," replied Ruth.

Miriam opened the little hatch to their attic room. The fire was still burning, making the room warm and cozy. On the big double bed, Miriam had laid out a stack of old photos, book entries, and other things to ponder over. "I have a lot of explaining to do. Why don't you come in, and sit a while."

In the rocking chair, Biddy Entwistle was dozing peacefully, her scarves wrapped loosely about her. The cats were nestled in her lap, and the smoldering fire cast a warm glow on their little cat faces.

"Biddy asked to hear one of my sleep poems," explained Miriam with a wink. She smiled again. "This way, we'll have plenty of time to talk, just you and me. And about the Witch stuff? Well, we'll see."

Miriam and Ruth, 2020

The End
(for now)

About the Author:

Mark Shoffner is an author and illustrator who lives his with his wife and daughter in San Francisco. This is his fourth book for children, and his first chapter book for younger readers.

OTHER BOOKS BY Mark Shoffner:

Call Me Haruki.

Haruki and the Laughing Cats

SNEEZUMS: The Sneeziest Cat in San Francisco

ESTORNUDOS: El Gato de San Francisco (in Spanish)